DRAKKYNN

DRAKKYNN

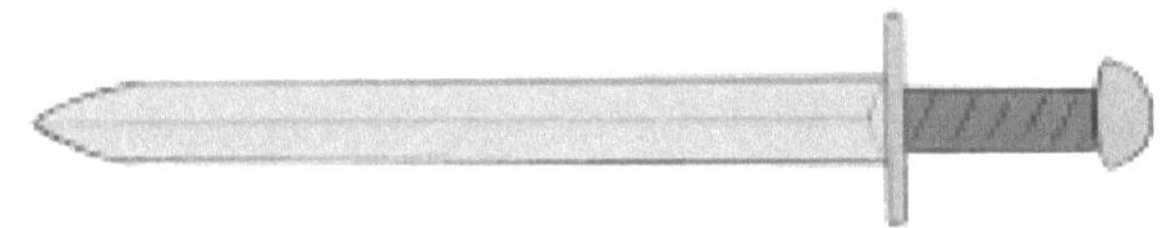

MATTHEW MCNEAL

Copyright © 2023 by Matthew McNeal

All rights reserved. No part of this publication may be reproduced, distributed, or transmitted in any form or by any means, including photocopying, recording, or other electronic or mechanical methods, without the prior written permission of the copyright owner and the publisher, except in the case of brief quotations embodiedin critical reviews and certain other noncommercial uses permitted by copyright law. For permission requests,write to the publisher, addressed "Attention: Permissions Coordinator," at the address below.

CITIOFBOOKS, INC.
3736 Eubank NE Suite A1
Albuquerque, NM 87111-3579
www.citiofbooks.com
Hotline: 1 (877) 389-2759
Fax: 1 (505) 930-7244

Ordering Information:
Quantity sales. Special discounts are available on quantity purchases by corporations, associations, and others. For details, contact the publisher at the address above.

Printed in the United States of America.

ISBN-13:   Softcover   978-1-962366-34-2
                eBook   978-1-962366-35-9
                Hardback   978-1-962366-36-6

Library of Congress Control Number: 2023918410

TABLE OF CONTENTS

DRAKKYNN

CHAPTER I

The Blackhawk helicopter skimmed above the thick canopy of the South American jungle. It was hopelessly searching, trying to visualize some sign or trace of the special military team that was scheduled to be in the area awaiting evacuation. The cockpit was black with hundreds of instruments and displays creating the only light, up until this point. Dawn was just breaking; the orange glow seeped out from the darkness creating a distinct separation between the passing night and the new day's horizon.

"I've got smoke at three o'clock!" exclaimed the copilot, pointing out at a plume of smoke a few thousand yards to the right of the chopper. In this endless sea of tropical vegetation, one stack of red smoke floated up from the dense green shell.

The pilot relayed the message. "Home base. This is SCOUT-TWO-FOUR-NINER. We have located smoke and suspect it may be the team down there. We are deploying a reconnaissance team to search for team members and any possible casualties. We will establish security for the surrounding perimeter. OVER."

"SCOUT-TWO-FOUR-NINER, We have received your message and we're dispatching a MEDIVAC, another

A-DETACHMENT, and we are alerting the NEST team. OVER."

"COPY THAT home base, we will recon and set up a perimeter while awaiting their arrival."

The first team member coupled to the rope and swung out of the helicopter and began his descent into the jungle. Each soldier touched the ground and positioned themselves several yards away from the landing zone so they could observe the next soldier coming down and still maintain a visual of the objective site. As the reconnaissance team rappelled down from the helicopter through the dense canopy, they could see the trees, shrubbery and ground; all scorched as if there had been a forest fire contained in this 50 square yard area. The ashes glowed with a greenish tinge and an eerie smell lingered throughout the area, similar to a type of burning that could not be categorized. The Geiger meters indicated only a faint level of radiation; the level that would be given of by the nuclear payload the team was carrying. Sergeant First Class Brune was the first soldier to hit the ground. He immediately started to scan the area, when he noticed a body in the distance. The body lay lifeless and smoldering in the haze.

" I've got a body." Yelled sergeant Brune, the senior medical sergeant. Sergeant First Class Brune moved towards the body and noticed chest movements and loud wheezing and rasping type breath sounds. He quickly turned to notify the other recon team members.

" He's alive, I don't know how, but he is." Sergeant Brune reached for the radio mic at his shoulder. Still looking for a way to identify the wounded soldier as he called for a medivac.

"COME IN MEDIVAC. This is sergeant first class Brune. We need immediate EVAC. Downed soldier with second to third degree burns over 75% of the body. Major burns on head, neck, face, and hands. Multiple lacerations and a left leg and right arm that are grossly deformed. REPEAT immediate EVAC!"

Sergeant Brune then kneeled down beside the soldier checking his airway and pulse. Brune quickly grabbed his medic bag and intubated the soldier due to the major burns, diminished respiratory rate, and respiratory distress. Next he started two 14 Gauge IV's and an infusion of Lactated Ringers. Too charred to decipher the nametape on the soldier's uniform, SFC Brune started to remove what was left of the soldiers' coat, slowly checking for any other injuries. There were three large slash marks going diagonally across the wounded soldier's chest approximately a foot in length and a half-inch in depth or more. These cuts, whatever their cause, severed the chain on the soldiers dog tags. SFC Brune found the ID tags lying inside of the coat. Sergeant Brune picked up the tags and wiped them off. The look on SFC Brunes face showed deep concern.

"SCOUT-TWO-FOUR-NINER. I've found him. I've found Colonel Allan. I need that MEDIVAC ASAP."

CHAPTER II

Mataxan City was a huge city flourishing with people from all races and religions. It lay on the coast and was a warm city with an economy based on tourism and natural resources. Also in the city was Mataxan Medical Center, one of the largest medical facilities in the world. Within the city were Fort Eagle and the Special Operations Center. In the center of the fort was the Hermann Command Center, where the steps of the mission had been overseen.

The conference room was long and desolate, enclosed in solid, white marble walls with two black steel doors on opposing ends. On the black doors was the NDS insignia. The main body had a green diamond with a red diamond inside of it. Two swords, one with a black and gold handle and the other with a turquoise and gold handle, were piercing down through the top of the diamond. In the center of the red diamond was a yellow sun with an orange and blue flame inside of it. Through the sun ran a black lightning bolt. In the middle of the room sat a long black smooth table covered with computer monitors, terminals, telephones, and fax machines. Clocks noting the different global cities and their current times lined the walls. A large screen built into the wall displayed an image of the globe, capable of pinpointing a small town and detailing it perfectly on the screen. On the opposite wall were huge glass windows that overlooked the numerous soldiers and technicians that operated the entire command center. Silent and calm lay the room.

The black steel doors burst open. "Can someone tell me what in the hell is going on?"

"General Sir, we're trying to figure that out right now!"

General Zorr was the commanding officer for all Special Operations Groups; this included the Army, Navy, Air Force, and the Marines. General Zorr was also head of the NDS. This was a group of highly specialized military personnel. Gathered from all branches of the military, each soldier had at the minimum of two Special Operations Qualifications, air operation training, SCUBA qualifications and sniper training. In his late 50's, General Zorr was taller than average with a large build. He had gray hair and a face that had been hardened through battle after battle. A Green Beret, Army Ranger, and Navy SEAL; an accomplishment few men have ever done, was one of the reasons he was the commanding officer of the SOG's. Thirty years of command experience were behind General Zorr and another thirty ahead, as far as he was concerned.

" What is the status on those troops?" The general slammed his hand down on the table.

" Eleven dead." One of the Generals advisors replied.

" Out of a twelve man A-team there is one survivor and we don't even have the foggiest notion of what occurred at that site."

" No, Sir"

" Who is the survivor?"

" Colonel Allan, Sir."

" If I had to expect one, it would be him."

" Sir."

" Yes."

" They don't expect Colonel Allan to make it through the night. When they found him, he was barely breathing and had second and third degree burns over 75% of his body with multiple other critical injuries."

" Take me to him, now!"

***

General Zorr was being led down a long corridor, which lead to the military's top-secret underground section of Prichard Memorial Hospital and Genetic Research Institute. There were heavy steel doors every ten feet and at least two guards, quite often four, at each door. Each soldier was a Green Beret fully armed and battle ready. At the end of the long corridor was a large set of double doors, engraved with radiation and biohazard marks. As the General entered the room he surveyed all of the surgical and life support equipment prepared to help Colonel Allan if his condition should decline. The General then quietly walked over to the bedside of Colonel Allan and threw back the curtain. The General starred at the corpse like body that was attached to the multiple types of monitoring equipment. For a few seconds the General quietly breathed.

"My God. What? How? I mean good lord what did this?"

Colonel Allan was almost covered from head to toe in burnt, cracked, dry brown skin. His eyes looked gray and dead. His lips were a dusky blue and his body's core temperature was 86 degrees Fahrenheit. The three large slashes on his chest, were black and deep into the tissue even scraping into bone. These slashes were accompanied by similar marks on his legs and

6

abdomen. On his right shoulder was an area that resembled flesh that had been mauled by a large carnivore, and one similar on his right leg. The EKG read a slow irregular heart rate in the 30's with constant irregular beats and runs of ventricular tachycardia. The Swan-Ganz catheter displayed a continuous cardiac output that was well below normal. The Colonel was on a ventilator to provide the desperately needed oxygenation that his own lungs could not provide. There was a chest tube on both sides of Colonel Allan's chest. His left leg was in traction and his right arm which had been crushed was in a cast. The foley catheter at his bedside had a bloody drainage instead of urine. Multiple IV fluids and blood products were infusing through large central venous catheters that had been placed in his right and left subclavian veins.

" Is he going to live?" the General turned to the team of doctors, headed by Dr. Cart.

Dr. Cart was a thin man of normal stature with dark hair and eyes. He had been a doctor for the military for 20 years and was a Brigadier General, but was by no means set in military ways. Specializing in critical care and trauma, Dr Cart had seen and treated almost every possible type of injury known to man. This is why he was requested to head the treatment and care of Colonel Allan. Dr. Cart also did research for the military, smart enough to do anything and knowing almost everything

" Sir, we don't know how he has survived this long."

"Did the nuclear payload his team was carrying cause these burns?"

" No."

" And what are these cuts or marks on his arms and legs? And why is there always three of them grouped together!?"

"We don't know sir. From what we can tell it wasn't a blade of any type"

" Then doctor can I ask this? Is there any part of Colonel Allan's problem that you can enlighten me on?"

Dr. Cart quickly looked at the General with a calm but fearless gaze.

"Sir, all we know is that Colonel Allan is alive. That, in it's self, is the most unusual and amazing part of this situation. And unless Colonel Allan survives this night and is able to regain some of his health, which is highly unlikely, neither you nor anyone else will ever know what happened to him or his team." Dr. Cart stated firmly.

General Zorr turned to walk away, then quickly stopped.

" Forgive my rudeness doctor. Please notify me of any changes as soon as they occur."

***

It was almost midnight and Dr. Cart was still at the hospital going over Colonel Allan's worsening lab results and vital signs.

" This is ridiculous and torturous." Dr. Cart said. "Major Neal"

"Yes. Dr. Cart." Said Major Neal, he was a shock/trauma nurse for the military.

"Major Neal. His condition is constantly deteriorating and I know he is in pain. From here on out; comfort measures only. Start a morphine, ativan, and diprivan drips, monitor his EKG rhythm, arterial blood pressure and pulse oximetry, and we will probably take him of the ventilator in the morning. Just let the monitor record the vital signs till morning and call me if something major happens."

"No problem Dr. Cart. If anything comes up I'll let you know."

As the night passed on Major Neal watched the monitors and titrated the pain and sedation medications to keep the Colonel comfortable. A little after five in the morning Major Neal glanced at the monitor and noticed that Colonel Allan's heart rate had jumped from the 30's to the 120's , his blood pressure that had been in the 90's over the 20's quickly dropped into the 30's over the 10's, and his pulse oximetry had dropped from 92% to 75% and was continuing to drop. Suddenly a loud thud was followed by a crash. Major Neal ran to the Colonels bedside. Colonel Allan had already pulled the endotracheal tube from his throat. As the ventilator was alarming Major Neal yelled for the technician to come help him to restrain Colonel Allan. Before the technician could get to the bedside Colonel Allan's right arm flexed and slammed against the side rail, shattering the cast that covered his almost completely crushed arm. With his right hand Colonel Allan reached up to his left shoulder as Major Neal was trying to hold his left arm down. His right hands' fingers dug into the thick charred skin that covered the Colonels shoulder and rest of his body. A large section of skin from his shoulder across his chest and half way down his abdomen peeled of like a section of armor would be removed by a knight. Underneath that hard section of skin lay pale mottled skin. The strength Colonel Allan held was remarkable, neither the Major nor the technician could come close to holding him still. Major Neal looked at the technician.

"Call Dr. Cart and tell him I said he needs to get here now!"

"It's burning!" Colonel Allan said with a hoarse shallow voice.

Colonel Allan continued to pull sections of hard charred skin from his body as if he was taking off sections of clothing. Reaching towards his left leg, Colonel Allan grabbed his knee with his left hand and the traction bar in the right hand and pulled with one quick motion, snapping the traction bar that was drilled through his leg. As the weights from the traction slammed to the ground, Major Neal and the technician starred in disbelief. Suddenly the Colonel grabbed a chest tube in each hand and pulled them clean from his chest, letting out a yell and slowly laying back in bed. Lifting his head up and looking at the Major and the technician, Colonel Allan said.

"I'm pretty tired now; I think I'll take a nap before breakfast." Colonel Allan then passed out. Major Neal and the technician placed EKG leads, SpO2 monitor, and a blood pressure cuff on Colonel Allan. All of his vital signs were normal.

***

That next morning, the General sat in his office, a large room with books on tactics, survival, philosophy, and ancient warriors. His desk was an old wooden desk that had been through most of the Generals career, showing signs of a battle-scarred history. General Zorr reviewed the maps, time hacks, and possible delays to the mission. Colonel Allan and his team were to infiltrate a terrorist group in the jungles of Argentina. There they would retrieve a new type of nuclear device that had been stolen from the British government. This device was the smallest yet most powerful nuclear device ever created. It was approximately ten inches long, eight inches wide, and two inches thick and could produce a blast of 140 megatons through numerous chain reactions moving from fusion to fission

As he reviewed the terrain maps, General Zorr talked himself through the steps of the mission.

"At 2100 hours the team executed a HALO jump which put them approximately six clicks south of their objective. The infiltration was to take place here, at 2330 hours. The team then moved 14 clicks north to the rendezvous point, here. The EVAC was to take place at 0600 hours. Radio contact was never reestablished after the teams 0100 hour check in. At 0800 hours, the search team located Colonel Allan's group. What happened in the hours between 1am and 8 am is a mystery, and I don't think anyone will ever know what really happened. The topographical maps show dormant volcanoes and rocky terrain. If the team stumbled on to a volcanic vent, that could explain the burns and the rocky terrain would account for some of the injuries. The slash marks? What about the slash marks? Maybe an animal. The area is deep in a little explored section of jungle. Possibly a wolf or a panther. No, that would be four cuts. A reptile of some type! That's it. Hot rocky terrain would be the perfect type of area for a reptile, but a reptile of that size would surely be known."

BZZZZZ. BZZZZZ. The General reached for his phone.

"General Zorr."

"General, this is Dr. Cart."

"Yes, Doctor."

"General, there has been a change in Colonel Allan condition. You need to get here now!"

CHAPTER III

General Zorr moved through the corridor and down to the ICU where Colonel Allan was being treated. He slammed through the doors shattering the silence of the unit. Before the doors could shut, Dr Cart was at his side already starting to brief him on the situation. "You're not going to believe this." Dr. Cart said with a look of astonishment and confusion.

"What is it?" Replied General Zorr.

"It's Colonel Allan."

"Did he die? Did his condition worsen?" General Zorr asked with a look of defeat.

"No. Colonel Allan is doing well."

"You called me down here because he's doing well?" General Zorr stated, sounding as if to say I was in the middle of something important.

"Let me show you how well, General." Dr. Cart said with a smirk.

When General Zorr walked around the curtain, he stopped dead in his tracks. He stood and stared in astonishment and disbelief. Colonel Allan was sitting at the edge of the bed talking to the nurses and doctors. No burns. No long deep cuts. Only scar tissue and pale skin in the place of the damage. Colonel Allan looked and acted as if he had never been on the mission, let alone injured.

"What in Gods name?"

"We've been trying to figure out why this happened. Well more to the point of how this happened. His vital signs are normal; all lab results are within normal limits except for his blood sugar is a little low, which is probably due to the accelerated healing process. Blood tests normal, urine tests normal, EKG is normal; there is no sign that Colonel Allan was ever that critically injured. Few scars. No broken bones. Little damaged tissue. Almost completely healed"

"Does he remember what happened?"

"We were waiting for you, Sir, before we asked."

"Excellent. You and I will be the only people in here when he explains what happened. Everything about this mission is top secret."

As the General and Dr. Cart moved around the curtain towards Colonel Allan's bed, the General gave a sign to one of the guards. The guard quickly cleared everyone from the room.

"Colonel Allan."

Colonel Allan sharply turned to General Zorr. Colonel Connor Allan was five foot ten and weighed about 225 lbs.; he had brown hair and green eyes and was in desperate need of a shave. Colonel Allan was one of the first members of the NDS. A Green Beret and Army Ranger who had just completed SEAL school before leaving for this last mission, Colonel Allan was one of the most highly trained soldiers the military had ever seen. The Colonel had a BS in chemistry and a Doctorate in Engineering. Trained as a sniper, skilled in basic field surgery and emergency medical techniques, and capable of infiltration through the air or by the water; were just some of Colonel Allan's refined military skills. He had been commanding troops for over 15 years and had never failed in accomplishing a mission. He always showed his team the utmost respect and trust. His team was the best because they all functioned as one, never making a mistake.

"Yes, Sir." Quickly snapping a salute.

"Carry on." The General returned the salute. "How are you feeling Colonel?"

"Fine, sir. I am pretty hungry, but I'm not in any pain or anything like that."

"Colonel Allan, when can you tell us about the mission and what happened to you and your men."

"Everything I remember Sir – and whenever you would like me to start."

"Please begin, if you feel up to it."

"Well, Sir, we made are HALO jump at approximately 2050 hours. As soon as my team hit the ground, we did a quick check of equipment and supplies incase anything was lost or damaged in the jump. We then proceeded to our objective and arrived at 2230 hours almost an hour ahead of our planned time. We then scouted the area to begin the recovery of the "nuke". We placed claymores and mines, and then set our firing patterns and sectors. After a quick radio check we initiated the recovery. There were 37 men at that site guarding the bomb. We first deployed the claymores; next we took out the three guard towers. We then moved forward eliminating the enemy force and recovering the nuclear device. Through the firefight Warrant Officer Smits was injured by small arms fire in his right shoulder. The nuclear weapon was recovered without any other injuries or loss of equipment."

"The NEST team recovered the "nuke," without any damages, from the transfer shielding your team was carrying it in." The General informed Colonel Allan.

"We then proceeded to the rendezvous point. On the way there, strange things started to happen. First, the temperature began to rise as it became later in the night. The temperature went from about 70 degrees up to around, I would say, 110 or higher. To begin with I thought it was because of the speed of our movement and the terrain, but it was the environment that was getting hotter. Then around 0100 hours we made our radio check. Around an hour later the radio started to malfunction and went dead. We couldn't find any mechanical reason for the malfunction in the equipment. At about 0330 hours there was a painfully loud explosion across the valley and on the next ridge. The blast concussion knocked us all to the ground. The noise was deafening and it disoriented all of the team for a short while. From what I could see it was a volcano, only it had a lava spout of about 30 feet in diameter, small for what I thought a volcano would be. It was the most amazing thing I had ever seen General. There wasn't any large cloud of ashes and rock spouting into the air, and the lava had an eerie greenish glow, yet the lava itself was yellow to red in color. The other thing was that we were all alive and this eruption had take place only half to three-quarters of a mile away."

"And this caused the burns on you and the rest of your team?" Dr. Cart asked with a look of enlightenment.

"No."

"Then how…."

"Dr., let him continue." General Zorr quickly interrupted.

"As we moved on, a dense haze settled in. I assume it was caused by the eruption. The strange thing was it was a greenish-gray haze with a strange burning smell."

"What kind of smell?" Dr. Cart asked.

"That is the strange thing about the smell, it was just a burning smell that none of us could pinpoint. At this point we were about 2 clicks away from the rendezvous point. We had stopped and set up a perimeter to take a rest and double check our location, equipment, and the payload we were carrying. We were also looking at the map to determine the best place for our pickup by the choppers. When all of the sudden we were under attack."

"Was it the terrorists trying to retake the nuclear weapon?"

"No, Sir, whatever it was didn't use any type of firearm."

"Whatever it was?" The General said with a puzzled look.

"Yes, Sir, I wasn't able to identify the aggressor. I do know it took out every member of my team one man at a time, with lethal precision that I had never seen before. There would be fire blasts here and gunfire there, but never a confirmed hit on the aggressor. Each man was taken out by a combination of being burnt and massive tissue damage with some type of a three-bladed weapon. This continued for thirty minutes until I seen a large blur coming directly at me and then I blacked out."

"Could you make out the blur?" General Zorr and Dr. Cart asked simultaneously.

"No, all I remember is that it was taller and wider than any man I had ever seen."

"Is there anything else you can tell us now Colonel?"

"No, General that's all I can remember."

"Well, all right, thank you Colonel. I'm going to leave now so the Dr. can finish running your tests and get you out of here. We will continue a debriefing later this week."

"As soon as the doctor clears me General, I will notify you."

"Yes." Dr. Cart started to assess Colonel Allan. "We have a few more tests to run before you go. I have to draw some blood since you pulled everything out last night."

As Dr. Cart wiped the alcohol pad over the vein on Colonel Allan's arm he noticed a sudden hardening. Thinking it must be because of the burn injuries, he proceeded with the blood draw. When he proceeded to stick the needle into Colonel Allan's arm, the skin instantaneously turned a dark greenish-brown with a diamond pattern that had a raised center. The needle bent and never even scratched the surface.

General Zorr, Dr. Cart, and especially Colonel Allan looked at each other in confusion and awe.

CHAPTER IV

Breaking the silence, Colonel Allan looked at Dr. Cart. "By any chance, can you explain to me what just happened?"

"No, I can't." The doctor said, with a confused laugh and a look of confusion engraved on his face. He then grabbed Colonel Allan's other arm and attempted to draw the blood. First he wiped the arm with the alcohol pad, and then proceeded to draw the blood. This time the needle slid easily into the Colonels arm and the blood was drawn with ease.

"I don't guess anyone could tell me why it happened and then why it didn't happen, and more than anything, why it happened in the first place?" Colonel Allan said with a kind of smart alick look on his face.

"Well…" Dr. Cart murmured. "No." With a confused laugh, again.

"Is there anything you CAN tell me? Even if it is a guess, I would like some idea about what my "diagnosis" is."

"I don't know…"

"You keep saying that!" Colonel Allan snapped.

"Let me run some tests. They're basic tests so they can be quickly done. Maybe they'll answer some of our questions."

"Some of our questions answered would be nice wouldn't you say Colonel?" The General said with a confused instead of stunned look.

"Nurse!" Called Dr. Cart.

"Yes, Doctor?" The nurse replied once the guard let the staff back into the unit.

"Please get me a scalpel set, two test tubes, spinal tap kit, and something to take fingernail and hair samples with."

"Right away doctor."

As soon as the nurse brought the equipment back, the doctor began to take the samples. Dr. Cart started to take the first skin sample while Colonel Allan was talking to the nurse about his blood pressure. There were no problems and the skin didn't make any changes. Dr. Cart placed the first sample in a test tube, then began to take the next sample.

"Colonel Allan, instead of from your hand lets take a skin sample from your forearm."

"No problems here Doc." Watching the procedure.

When Dr. Cart started to remove the skin with the scalpel, the area turned into the same dark greenish-brown pattern as before.

"Dr. Cart?"

"Yes Colonel, Yes. Let's continue with the tests. We'll do the spinal tap next."

"Alright Colonel, if you can roll over on your side we'll get the sample." Colonel Allan positioned himself on the bed. "Try to put your chin close to your chest. It makes getting the sample easier. This is going to sting a bit."

As the words rolled out of Dr. Cart's mouth, the skin all along Colonel Allan's back turned dark greenish-brown with the same diamond pattern as had appeared on his arm. At his spine formed a raised area with the same pattern, with larger raised centers. The raised center of these scales, as they seemed, increased in size from the outer back in towards the spine. At the spine the raised centers took on more of a horn like resemblance. They were about an inch high at the lower back and increased in size to about three inches at the base of the neck. On these center horns or spikes that protruded from the Colonels back, was an even stranger site. At the tip of each spike was a smooth green rock looking substance. This point looked like a diamond except it was a dark green, not greenish brown like the scales but a bright dark green. Dr. Cart stood and stared, not with a look of confusion but of enlightenment. At this point he decided to prove the theory that he had.

"What's wrong doctor?" Said General Zorr, unable to see what was happening.

"Colonel Allan, would you please stand up?" Focusing on the Colonel instead of General Zorr's Question.

"Yes, Doctor." Colonel Allan sat up, and then stood at the side of his bed.

"Colonel, hold your left arm out please."

As Colonel Allan held his arm out, Dr. Cart made a stabbing motion with the scalpel towards his arm, as if to cut his arm completely off.

"What in the hell are you doing!?" The Colonel shouted as he yanked his arm back behind him.

"Have you gone mad!?" General Zorr yelled at the doctor with a look of massive confusion.

"Colonel, please hold your arm back out." Dr. Cart calmly requested as he placed the scalpel at the bedside table.

"No!" Colonel Allan exclaimed angrily.

"Just do it." Dr. Cart calmly said.

Moving his arm out from behind him, Colonel Allan and General Zorr looked in astonishment. The Colonel's entire arm was covered with the dark greenish-brown scales. On the elbow was a large spike, about four inches long and similar to the ones that formed on his back during the preparation for the spinal tap. The spike protruded out as if it were attached to the bone in his forearm and was tipped with the same jewel like rock. His hands had undergone a change as well, instead of four fingers there were only three. The two middle fingers appeared as if they had fused together. At the end of each finger and thumb jutted out a claw that looked similar to the composition of the spike on the elbow. The palm of the hands had a different look than the rest of the skin. They had a dark tan color and had what looked like bands across them. The bands were approximately a quarter of an inch wide and looked as if the side towards the wrist of each band had a knife like edge to it. The knuckles had also formed spikes, except there were only three spikes, the same number as the fingers. The middle spike was about two inches long and the outer spikes about one inch each, similar in composition and form to the spikes on the elbow and back.

"I don't understand doctor." Colonel Allan stated with a look of fear and astonishment.

"I noticed it when I was going to perform the spinal tap." Dr. Cart said confidently.

"Noticed what?" General Zorr questioned.

"It's a response to the threat of injury. Think about it every time you were not paying attention the samples were taken without any problems. But, every time you watched or were anticipating pain or injury your body reacted to protect itself. Not in a manner as extreme as your arm, but enough to prevent harm. Look at your arm now."

Colonel Allan looked down at his arm and it began to transform back to the normal human arm. The scales slowly disappeared, changing into soft, smooth, pink skin. Each of the spikes receded back into the bones they extended from. The knuckle spikes receded as well, and the second and third fingers separated from the one large finger into the normal shape of a hand. The bands on the palm of his hand faded into the pinkish-tan flesh that normally belonged there. The rigidity and coarseness that had only moments ago covered the Colonels arm was nowhere to be seen.

"Well now we know why it does this, but I would like to know how it occurs and what caused it." Colonel Allan said, with not quite the same enthusiasm as Dr. Cart was showing.

"We'll run the tests on those skin samples. That should tell us something." Dr. Cart said with a look of astonishment and excitement.

CHAPTER V

It was 9:00 A.M. the next day before Dr. Cart returned with the results of the tests. Dr. Cart walked into the unit with a strange grin and an enthusiastic pace. The look on his face showed that he had found many things out, but was left with many more questions.

"What can you tell me?" Colonel Allan quickly inquired.

"First, your cells are growing; well, I should say regenerating at a rate I have never seen before."

"What do you mean by regenerating and not growing?"

"When you take cells and place them in a medium, cells start to multiply. The medium is the nutrient filled substance we place the cells in to promote growth. Since they were skin cells, they would reproduce duplicates of themselves. Now then again, it isn't a lot. Usually the cells double maybe once or possibly twice before they die, but your cells had a twist. The cells I removed from your skin did not multiply; instead they would take what nutrients were in the medium and repaired themselves. If the cell wall weakened or broke, the cells literally rebuilt it with the help of the surrounding cells. When one of the cells could not be repaired because of too much damage, the other cells broke that cell down and produced another cell to take its place. It is similar to disassembling a vehicle and reusing good parts and replacing worn or useless parts to produce a same as new vehicle. That, I thought, was how the burns that covered your body healed so quickly." Dr Cart explained in triumph.

"What do you mean by "thought" doctor?" Colonel Allan asked curiously, and looking puzzled.

"I noticed that the cells either repaired themselves or the healthy cells broke down the weak or dying cells and created a replacement. So I divided the sample into two different containers and subjected one of them to tests and I left the other as the control group. First, I added high levels of heat, which started to kill the cells on the outer areas of the sample. I then removed the heat and the cells regenerated themselves in about a half-hour. With the next test I added more heat for a longer period of time almost destroying all of the cells. When I observed the cells after about five minutes they had all regenerated back to normal."

"I don't understand what you're getting at doctor." Replied Colonel Allan.

"I'm trying to say that the worse the injury is, the faster your body regenerates itself. So if you were to place a cut on each of your arms, one being four inches long and the other two, the four inch cut would be healed in either the same amount or less time than the two inch cut."

"So the longer cut would heal itself in a couple of days as well as the shorter cut?" The Colonel questioned.

"Yes, only it would be more like hours instead of days."

"What else did you find doctor?" Almost afraid to ask.

"Your cells are also immune to any type of poisoning, at least what we were capable of testing. Your cells were not affected by any changes in the level of oxygen or carbon dioxide. They grew in 100% carbon dioxide just as well as in 100 % oxygen. They also survived in any type of medium we placed them in, whether it be water, nutrients, or toxic materials.

"What do you mean they survived in any medium? Do they form a shell to protect themselves like my arm did?"

"No, no, Colonel. What I mean is they use whatever the medium is. They absorb and live on the medium, and that's why we don't believe your cells can be affected by poison or toxic substance. We also ran tests on your blood. First, your red blood cells pick-up oxygen as normal, but they also store oxygen indefinitely and use it as needed. Next, your white blood cells are at the normal count, when they should be extremely high from the injuries that you had. I'm going to assume that due to the regeneration capabilities your body has your white blood count will never be high. And last but definitely not least, you have a new type of blood cell. This new blood cell, from what I can figure is why your cells can survive so well. This cell, we'll call it 3CELL, takes any foreign or toxic substance floating around in the blood stream and absorbs it. It then breaks the substance down, releasing usable materials. If it cannot use the material it ingests it and then changes it into a usable material. It would be like breaking down a piece of wood and rearranging the atoms to create gold." All of this Dr. Cart was saying with a smile as if he had just found his best friend.

"I am glad you find all of this amusing doctor, but can you now tell me in layman's terms what is going on and how to fix it." Colonel Allan said with a bit of agitation in his voice.

"What is going on is that your body can regenerate almost indefinitely, and you are immune to all infections, diseases, and toxins. How to fix it, I don't know. It seems permanent from the tests we ran."

"What do you mean by permanent?" The Colonel said as he stared at Dr. Cart.

"By "permanent," I mean if your body doesn't loose the ability to regenerate, you're going to live a very long time."

"Define long doctor!" Colonel Allan said with a look of unamusement.

With a look of seriousness Dr. Cart replied. "Two or three thousand years, maybe longer. I would venture to say that you are the closest thing to immortality that the world has ever seen." A blanket of silence fell over the two men. Neither man knowing what to say or do. As time passed thoughts ran through both of the men's minds.

"This could be a blessing or a curse."

"No disease or death."

"I'll have to see all my loved ones die."

"Will it ever end?"

"What about continuing with life?"

"Will the military exploit him?

Breaking the silence, Dr Cart asked. "Are you up to performing some physical tests?"

"Yes. I've got to do something."

As the two men walked down the hall, silence still surrounded them. The guards, all knowing Colonel Allan, saluted him. The Colonel and the doctor turned left at the end of the corridor. At the end was a gymnasium; it had weight lifting equipment, a swimming pool, and even an indoor track, everything that could be thought of to deal with fitness.

"I would like to test you on some of your physical capacities and then check them with prior records." Dr. Cart requested kindly.

"That's fine with me doctor but I'm positive everything will be low because of my injuries and what's happened over the past few days."

"I agree with you, but I can also use them as a gage in you recovery. So let's begin."

CHAPTER VI

Along black limousine pulled up to the entrance of the hospital. General Zorr stepped out of the limousine and quickly walked to the elevators in the lobby. He had been in briefings all morning about the mission Colonel Allan was leading and what had happened at the rendezvous. He gave all the details he had from his records and also what Colonel Allan had described to him. Many questions had been asked about the strange attack and also the status of Colonel Allan's health, few General Zorr was able to provide a clear picture for. Answering as many questions as he could, the General knew he would have to wait and talk to Dr. Cart and Colonel Allan in more detail.

"KNOCK! KNOCK! KNOCK!"

"Come in." Dr. Cart looked up as the door opened and General Zorr walked in. "Hello, General, can I help you?"

"Yes, Doctor. I was wondering if you could tell me anything more about Colonel Allan's condition?"

"I have a lot to tell you General." Dr. Cart said to General Zorr as he got up and locked the door.

" I know quite a bit of Colonel Allan's mission was top secret, and what I have to tell you should be kept between me, you, and the Colonel."

"Did you find out anything about his recovery doctor?" The General asked with a look of intensity.

"Yes, that and much more." Dr. Cart said with a slight laugh.

"Well, don't keep me waiting doctor."

"First, from what we know Colonel Allan's body has been altered in some way. He is able to regenerate his body at exceptional speeds, and I don't mean heal his body. If you were to remove a section of skin and muscle from his arm, his body would replace it within a matter of hours. You could cut off one of his fingers and it would be there the next day."

"That's impossible." The General said as if it were a joke.

"No, it isn't sir. Plus there's more. His blood has a new type of blood cell. This new cell absorbs any toxic or harmful material, releases what is usable back into the bloodstream, and then changes the unusable material into usable material. This means he is immune to all disease, infection, or poison. And you were there when we figured out the transformation his body undertakes to protect it's self."

"What could have caused his body to do this? There are too many science fiction movies out there about things like this, but oh well I'll ask anyway. Was it from the radiation?

"Sir, we're not sure what caused this. That is the one thing I'm trying to find out. Oh, there are some other things I wanted to tell you. I had Colonel Allan to take some physical tests to see how they compared with his prior records. I could also use them to gage his recovery. These were the results."

2 mile run	time: 7min. 38 sec.
Bench press	max weight: 460 lbs.
Squat	max weight: 2012 lbs.

"Those weights and times are impossible doctor." The General said with a look of disbelief.

" I thought the same thing General, but two hours later he ran the two miles and took almost ten seconds off of his previous time. The Colonel's best time in a two mile run was 11: 30, and if I had not been there I would not have believed it either."

"What about the weights doctor? Those are remarkable feats even for a man in peak physical condition like Colonel Allan."

"That is true General, but, those weights are where I made him stop. Each of those weights he did ten times. And I don't mean ten separate times, he did one set of ten for each of those weights."

"What does all this mean Dr. Cart?"

"It means that what ever happened to Colonel Allan affected many things and I don't think we know the half of them."

"Can I go talk to the Colonel now?"

"Yes General that's where I was heading before you came in. He's is in the gym right now."

General Zorr and Dr. Cart left the office and headed for the elevator. As they walked towards the elevator, the General kept thinking that all of this was a hoax. The transformation, the speed, and the feats of strength were all impossible. It must be the doctor fixing all of the scores and situations. But why? I was present when the skin transformed, so I can't explain that.

Here at the gym, thought the General I'll see what's true and what's not. The elevator doors opened, and Dr Cart and General Zorr stepped out. Colonel Allan was just walking off of the track, where he had just ran five miles, and heading for the free weights.

"Colonel Allan?" General Zorr yelled. "Could you run a mile and let me time it please?" General Zorr figured if he could run that fast, why would it matter, even if he had just finished running.

"No problem sir." Colonel Allan said with a smirk on his face.

Colonel Allan started running. It was a fast pace, almost a sprint or a dead run. He stayed at the same pace throughout the entire run. As Colonel Allan came around the track on his fourth lap, General Zorr looked down at his stopwatch.

"3:01…3:02…3:03…3:04…3:05…3:06. He just did the mile run in three minutes and six seconds. How is that possible doctor?

"We don't know General Zorr. There is a catch, though."

"A catch?" General Zorr said with a look of uncertainty. "Of course there's a catch! What is it?"

"Yes, he keeps getting faster. Plus his ability to swim has improved."

"He is an excellent swimmer already doctor, I mean, he is a SEAL." General Zorr said sarcastically.

"Yes he was an excellent swimmer…. Why don't I just show you what I mean General? Colonel Allan?"

"Yes, Doctor?" The Colonel looked up from the floor where he was stretching.

"Are you ready to swim some laps?"

"I'll meet you at the pool doctor. I need to go change into my trunks."

As Colonel Allan walked into the locker room, General Zorr and Dr. Cart headed towards the pool. They walked across the gym, passing free weights and other exercise equipment. There were ropes for climbing and equipment for gymnastics training. On the other side of the gym was a tunnel, this tunnel led to the pool. The closer the General and Dr. Cart came to the tunnel, the greater the smell of chlorine became. The heat and humidity increased, as was expected. The two men entered the pool area and waited for Colonel Allan. A few minutes later Colonel Allan came to the pool with his trunks on and a towel. No sign of the burns or cuts could be seen on his body. He looked just as conditioned as the day he graduated from Ranger school, well muscled and cut like a bodybuilder.

"How far would you like me to swim today, doctor?" The Colonel asked as he climbed the stairs to the diving board.

"How about a mile and see how fast you can go. We won't time you but let's show the General how you have improved." Dr. Cart said with a smirk.

"That's fine with me doc." Colonel Allan smiled back at Dr. Cart.

Colonel Allan ran to the end of the springboard and jumped high into the air, diving gracefully into the pool. The Colonel started swimming his laps as anyone would, but as the General watched he noticed something happening. Colonel Allan's hands and feet turned green.

"Doctor, what's happening with Colonel Allan?"

"This is what I wanted to show you General. Colonel Allan! Colonel Allan!" The doctor caught the Colonel's attention.

"Yes, doctor?"

"Show the General your hands and feet."

Colonel Allan picked himself out of the pool and sat at the edge. His hands and feet were covered with the same dark greenish-brown pattern as before, except this time it was much smoother. His hands had three fingers as before but there was webbing between the fingers. The feet had taken on a completely different look. They were extended from the toes into the form of flippers and both of the heels had each formed into a dorsal fin like protrusion, making his legs more streamlined.

"How do these changes occur doctor?" General Zorr pondered out loud.

"We don't know General. What we do believe is that whatever obstacle is put in Colonel Allan's path, his body instantaneously adapts to negotiate the obstacle. What we do know is that the more Colonel Allan uses these skills; the better he is able to control them. Why don't you show him Colonel?"

"Alright doctor, I'll give it a try." Colonel Allan started to concentrate and relax. Slowly his hands and feet transformed from their aquatic state to his normal appendages.

"This is amazing." General Zorr said.

"I think it's enough for today doctor. I'm going to go eat and rest and I'll see you in the morning."

"That's fine Colonel, I'll see you tomorrow." Colonel Allan then turned and walked into the locker room. "Would you like to come tomorrow morning and watch some of the tests General?"

"Yes, Dr. Cart I would like that."

"Then I'll see you tomorrow, General."

CHAPTER VII

Grindolph International Airport was ten miles outside of Mataxan city. There were an enormous number of flights, international and domestic, in and out of the airport. The airport was equipped to handle any type of flight; military transports to private flights. Late at night, on a distant runway, a Leer Jet was descending for its landing. Inside the jet was one of the worst gatherings of criminals known to man. As the jet came to a halt, the passenger door opened and the jet way moved to the entrance. First to exit the jet was Braco Kinng, he was the leader of this mercenary group and was wanted by numerous countries for crimes against humanity. He was an obese man with white hair. His stature was short and look was of utter contempt and disgust for mankind. Never being caught had left a chip on his shoulder that could never be knocked off.

Braco looked down the stairs at the HUMVEE limousines that were awaiting him and his associates. Next to leave the plane was Kine and Demic. This pair had long worked with Braco, well known for their destructive capabilities and technological genius. Of normal height and stature, the men looked middle aged and in good physical condition. Both men having past military experience were now bought by the highest bidder. Each man was highly skilled in weapons and mortal combat. Neither of the three men knew who had hired them for the job they were arriving to do, but none were worried because their compensation was excellent.

Four more mercenaries exited the aircraft. Nayad, Rous, Hisk, and Thour; each hired for their excellence in a specific field. Nayad was an expert in demolitions and explosives. Rous was an ex-SAS pilot who could fly any aircraft made. Hisk, a weapons specialist could acquire any and all types of equipment in a short amount of time. Finally was Thour who had been a biological and chemical weapons expert and a MD before discovering the lucrative pay of his now chosen profession. Braco, Kine, and Demic climbed into the first limousine and the other men went to the other.

The group was taken across Mataxan city to the Griffin Hotel were their suites awaited them. In each man's room was a large silver briefcase, and enclosed was 20 million dollars in small bills. Also inside the case were directions to their meeting place.

Two hours later each man arrived at an abandoned wherehouse along the piers outside of Mataxan city. A large round table sat in the middle of the room. To the left was an open space that housed several vehicles, to be used by the men at the table. On the right was a large storeroom that contained weapons, ammunition, explosives, and communications equipment. The group gathered around the table.

"Please sit down gentleman." Said Braco. "Each of you has been hired for your unique abilities and your reputations, and not to mention your other qualities. The compensation at the hotel is at this minute being deposited into the International

Exchange Bank across the street. My employees are doing this so to attract less attention to each of you. Your money is being deposited into the offshore accounts that you have each designated. If you will open the cover to the laptop computers in front of you, you can check that the deposits have been made."

Each man checked his account and found the money in its designated account.

"Does anyone have any questions at this moment?" Braco asked. "No, then I will begin. We have been hired to recover a certain package from the Fort Eagle military installation."

"Certain package?" Demic inquired.

"More to the point, a nuclear package. This is not an ordinary nuclear device. It is the CUF36 bomb, which I believe Nayad can give us a more detailed description."

Nayad stood up from his seat. " The CUF36 is the most compact nuclear explosive known by man. It is approximately the same size as these computers in front of us. The only exception is that the bomb is about two inches thick. This bomb is capable of a 140-megaton explosion. This is due to the ability of a new nuclear component that was mistakenly discovered and is far more potent than plutonium. This component goes through the fission and fusion processes several times in a successive chain reaction."

Nayad slowly sat back into his seat.

"Thank you Nayad." Braco said as he stood up.

"Braco, I was informed that this nuclear device was retaken by the U.S. government and then lost in a firefight in the jungles of Argentina?" Kine asked.

"The firefight was correct, Kine, but the bomb was recovered and is in the Fort Eagle complex. And within the next six days we will retake the nuclear device. Planning will begin immediately. Any equipment that is not here that any of you need can be supplied within 24 hours. Vehicles that may be needed can be delivered also within 24 hours. Once the nuclear bomb is acquired, any equipment and vehicles are yours. Private jets have been chartered and will be awaiting your arrivals to depart to the countries you have each previously designated. Now, if there are no questions, I suggest we begin."

CHAPTER VIII

Colonel Allan was changing from his gym clothes into his civilian clothes.

"Where are you going?" Dr. Cart asked as he walked into the room that had recently became Colonel Allan's home.

"I, am going out."

"You can't do that."

"Why not?"

"There are more tests I need to run and samples to get."

"You have enough samples and test results to work on for the next couple of days while I go and visit my friends."

"But, But……."

"But if your aunt had balls she would be your uncle!" Colonel Allan exclaimed.

Dr. Cart looked confused at Colonel Allan. "What if something happens?"

"If anything happens I will call you immediately, Doc."

"Alright, two days, then be right back here. Please update me at least once a day to your condition and if your still feeling all right."

"No problem, you're the doctor!"

***

Colonel Allan pulled into the parking lot of a large building called EngKomTec Inc. Inside the building was an entire workshop where any type of equipment could be designed and built. The company was owned by Colonel Allan and his friend Jack Presson. Jack ran the company because Connor was constantly on assignment and never around.

"Hey Jack!"

"Holy shit?!" Jack said with relief. "All the damn military would tell me was that you had been injured. They wouldn't tell me if it was a minor injury, if you were damn near dead or if you were dead! I am ready to kick the shit out of that General of yours. It is really sad because I even worked with you all." Jack Presson was a former Major in the NDS and teammate of Connor's. He had been the intelligence officer and engineering technician. Once he had left the military, he and Connor began EngKomTec. This company designed and built anything.

Connor chuckled. "Of all people he would be the only person you would have any trouble fighting. But, I am glad they didn't tell you what had happened."

"Why?" Jack said.

"Because, I was almost dead, actually I don't know how I am here right now talking to you instead of being placed in a grave."

" What do you mean, you look perfectly fine to me."

" Now, I look normal." Connor snickered and mumbled under his breath. "Normal!!!"

"You had better quit mumbling and tell me what happened!"

"Alright, you know I can't tell you anything about the mission."

"Right, all the hush hush secret bullshit." Jack said sarcastically. "I remember from my stint."

" At the end of the mission, we ended up in a firefight, but it was one sided." Jack looked strangely at Connor. "Just let me try to explain as much as I can then you can ask questions. BELIEVE ME, you will have questions! We were under attack by something that moved like lightning and struck targets with as much damage. Whoever or whatever it was did not use any weapon other than some type of three bladed knife or something. Plus it had a type of flame thrower or napalm gun that was incinerating everything in its path, including my team and me. From that point on I don't remember a thing until I woke up at the hospital."

"If you were burned, how are you here instead of in the hospital and where are the burns."

"That comes later, first I am going to tell you how they found me. When the search team found my team, I was the only one alive. I was covered in second and third degree burns and had several sets of those slash marks from that three bladed knife or whatever it was. I was immediately flown out and to the hospital. At the hospital I was on the ventilator because my lungs were burnt, my heart rate was in the 20-30's, and I was pretty well dead."

"OK, this is definitely an interesting story and why you would make this up is beyond me?" Jack said, as he started to turn and walk away, disgusted with such a stupid story.

"Don't leave Jack, I am not lying and I will prove it when I am finished telling you everything else. Everything I told you about the hospital is in their records, because when I woke up I did not believe what they told me. I felt the same way you did, that this was all horseshit. Once I woke up, I was bombarded with questions I couldn't answer and tests that I couldn't understand. So for the next couple of days I was a giant guinea pig for their research.   Now, this is what they told me, somehow my body has gained the ability to regenerate parts, heal itself from any damage, and protect itself in a very unique way. A couple other things but they are kind of minor compared to everything else."

" I am still waiting for you to prove this wonderful story! Because it is pissing me off that you would expect me to believe such a story." Jack said furiously.

" I know it sounds like horseshit, but it is the truth. Here is your proof in two parts." Over the last several days Connor had become more and more in control of his ability to alter his body, instead of it being a reaction to a situation. Connor held his arm out and slowly the skin turned to a slight shade of green and became darker and darker. The diamond shape pattern with raised centers reappeared as it had done that first day. His elbow grew into the large bony spike and his fingers went from four to three with their razor sharp claws and their bony protrusions at the knuckles.

" Well, I'll give you credit, that is an impressive trick. So the military designed a portable hologram machine." Replied Jack.

" OK, feel my arm." Jack reached out and touched the scales and bony protrusions. " Does that feel like a Halloween fake arm made by a hologram?"

" No, but it still doesn't look real!"

" Well here is the second part of the proof. Do you have extra blades for that band saw right there?"

" Yeah, there in the back."

Connor walked over to the band saw and flipped the switch on. He then turned the speed to its highest level.

" What are you going to do with that?" Jack said with a bewildered look.

"This!" With his armored hand Connor quickly reached over and grabbed the blade of the band saw.

"STOP!?" Jack yelled knowing that Connors hand would be ripped to shreds. The band saw came to a dead stop and the fuse blew. Jack looked over to see Connor holding the band saw blade in his hand. No blood anywhere.

"I don't understand" Jack quickly moved to Connors side and opened his hand. The blade of the saw was mangled and dull, while Connors hand didn't have a scratch or nick anywhere. As Jack grabbed Connors hand he began to go over it inch by inch trying to bring some sanity to the situation. Jack touched the palm of Connors hand and he yanked his hand back. " Your hand feels like hot metal."

" All I felt was the initial jolt of when I caught the blade. No pain, No heat, No pressure."

" I don't understand how this is possible?"

" The sad thing is my friend, is that there is a lot more to tell you, and it gets more interesting."

" Well the shop is closed and you have got a lot of things to tell me, so let's go get a drink and eat."

CHAPTER IX

Dr. Cart sat in his office going over Colonel Allan's lab tests and his physical results. Dr. Cart's office was one large filing cabinet. There wasn't an uncluttered spot in the entire office. Every chair had a stack of papers and books, the cabinets were crammed full of files and changes of clothes. The bookshelves had numerous medical journals and great works of literature, mythology, and theology. The one and only organized area was the back of Dr. Cart's door. On the door was a giant sign that simply read " IF YOU WERE GOING TO DIE TOMORROW…..WHAT WOULD YOU DO TODAY!!!!!"

"KNOCK! KNOCK! KNOCK!"

" Come in."

General Zorr stuck his head around the door entering Dr. Carts' office.

"Yes, General? Can I help you?"

"Yes, Dr. Cart. I wanted to stop by and see how Colonel Allan was feeling and if you had found out anything else about his condition?"

"Well, Colonel Allan isn't here right now, he is at Jack Presson's."

"Are you crazy!? No one gave you permission to let that man off of the premises!" General Zorr began to yell.

"Look asshole, I have heard enough of your shit! You are in my world now, and my rules are taken into consideration far ahead of anyone else's. Yes I am military but I do not conform to your mindless horseshit. If you want to talk to me person to person no problem, but if you want to yell, you are going to get the hell out of my hospital. Now as it comes to Colonel Allan, he has more stress upon him at this moment than you or I will ever know. And as a Dr. I deem it necessary for him to visit with his friends and relax for a while." Dr Cart replied without breaking a stride.

General Zorr stood at the doorway with a look of disbelief and anger. No man had ever yelled at him in a way that left him with nothing to say.

"Now if you want to discuss things please come in." Dr. Cart said calmly.

"Is there anything new about the colonel's condition?"

"The main thing is his ability to adapt to any situation at uncharted speeds. The only other thing that is really new is that I do not know when this will wear off or if it will ever go away. I have also discussed with the colonel that if things do not change or reverse themselves, he is going to be the closest thing to immortality that the world has ever known."

"You are telling me that Colonel Allan can't be killed?" General Zorr smirked.

"No, I am not saying that he can't be killed, although anything I can think of would not be able to harm him. What I mean is that his body will constantly repair and regenerate itself and I don't have any reason from the tests we have conducted to see this capability disappearing."

"How is this possible, I have never heard of anyone being able to change their body to protect itself? Let alone someone who is immortal. These things only happen in myths and legends."

"How familiar are you with the legends of the werewolf?" Dr. Cart asked General Zorr.

"You mean all the hub-bub about being attacked by a wolf or wolf-like creature and whenever the full moon comes out, you start barking at the moon and sniffing your crotch!" General Zorr sarcastically replied.

"Yes, those legends." Dr. Cart said while laughing under his breath.

"Yes, I am familiar with those legends. I guess now you're going to tell me that Colonel Connor Allan was attacked by a werewolf like creature."

"Since the beginning of time, man has had legends of half animal half man creatures that terrorized civilization. The Sphinx of old mythology was a beautiful creature that killed with no remorse. The Minotaur was a creature with a man's body and a bull's head that roamed a great labyrinth, killing whoever entered. In Africa, there are the stories of wild man-beast creatures that resembled anything from crocodiles, lions, and jackals. Here in the United States, Sasquatch, the Native Americans have told stories of this creature for centuries."

"Yes Dr. Cart, myths and legends. No proof has ever been found to put any of these creatures in any type of book other than fiction."

"Of all these myths and legends that you have read or heard, were any of the creatures good or kind to man? No! In any of these stories the creatures are evil and cruel to mankind. Some way or another they are killing, destroying, or driving away man. Even in today's society, only the bad or evil things are the headlines for the papers. It is just a natural thing."

"What are you getting at doctor."

"As time has passed, science and technology have taken the world by storm. Myths and legends have been thrown to the side because they were disproved or no truth could be found in them. You know as well as I do that good and evil go hand in hand. If there was such a creature that was immortal and helped people all the time, no one would pay a lot of attention to them. It is like the difference between Hitler and mother Theresa. Both extremely famous, but both at opposite ends of a spectrum. One thought to be the antichrist and the other gave up everything to help people. Which one is easier to pick out in a conversation?"

"Hitler of course!" General Zorr said.

"Exactly! Why would these creatures want to be revealed. Instead why not hide in society or someplace you wouldn't have to deal with society. And wait!"

"Wait for what doctor?"

"Is it not possible that the creatures these myths were told about, have in a way been driven out of society and into hiding. Since these creatures were not evil, like their brethren of whom all these myths and legends were written, they quietly chose to remain hidden and dormant. Waiting for the time when society is tolerant of people or things that are different." Pausing for a second. "You have a lot of time when you're immortal."

"Personally, I think you're crazy." General Zorr quickly replied.

"All right now, think about this. In all religions and mythologies there is always good and evil, and always those that are torn between good and evil. The other thing is that when things first began to be written down it almost always dealt with the supernatural. For instance one of the first pieces of English literature is Beowulf. A creature of unbelievable strength and almost no vulnerabilities. It killed men by the dozens and lived deep in a swamp. In Greek and Roman mythology, deities and creatures of all kinds tried to destroy mankind while some tried to help mankind prosper. The bible tells of one-third of heavens angels rebelling and being cast into hell and from there they try to corrupt mankind. Then in our own history you have Vlad the Impaler, otherwise known as Dracula, Hitler, Jack the Ripper, and Rasputin."

"But those are men, not vampires or demons or fallen angels or even evil Greek or Roman myths." General Zorr said.

"Yes, but monsters none the same. No matter when evil has tried to overcome the world something has stopped it. Rasputin was poisoned; but when it didn't bother him they decided to riddle his body with bullets, throw him into an icy river, then buried him. Eventually he was exhumed and burned. Hitler was poisoned and burned after killing millions and trying to create a super race that he knew he wasn't even good enough for. Vlad Dracula impaled countless thousands to maintain his kingdom until he was finally caught, beheaded, and buried at a monastery. Later when his grave was to be exhumed, his body was never found. Jack the Ripper terrorized London by brutally murdering people yet disappeared without a trace. With all of this maybe they had a major evil influence."

"Are you trying to tell me that those four lunatics were possessed?"

"No, what I am trying to say is that maybe all the myths and legends have some truth to them."

"So you think vampires, werewolves, and demons really exist?" General Zorr said with a great deal of disbelief.

"What if they do? General, how well can you train the men you have under your command to conceal themselves, blend in as to not disturb or disrupt things. Now imagine a creature that has a human form, or shape shifts, or blends into its surroundings. Plus, thousands of years of experience. Would it or they be easy to find or even recognize if you bumped into them on the street."

"It's just not possible!"

"I can't tell you your wrong General, but if a vampire was dead, how would we tell it between another dead body. It is the undead. Werewolves turn back into there human form once they have been killed supposedly. Who is to say that a demon doesn't just burst into flames. That would make the body kind of hard to discern between human or unnatural."

"This is ridiculous Dr. Cart. Nothing even remotely like these creatures has been discovered."

Dr. Cart leans forward putting his arms on his desk. He begins to glare at General Zorr.

"What about Colonel Connor Allan?"

"Are you out of your mind? Colonel Allan is a US citizen, a soldier, sworn to protect this country and its freedoms. He isn't an evil creature hell bent on destroying the world."

"Your right, but how do you explain his abilities. Because we can't explain them medically. Well, medically and scientifically speaking, what he can do is impossible. The only thing that remotely explains his abilities is the word supernatural. And no, I don't believe he is an evil creature hell bent on destroying the world, but I think he may be in the same category as vampires, werewolves, and demons. I just think he may be part of the good in that world of good and evil we have been taught or convinced to believe doesn't exist."

CHAPTER X

Several days had passed and the mercenaries had devised their plan to infiltrate the Fort Eagle Complex. Once inside the complex they would break into the research centers security compound. Braco Kinng, Kine, Demic, and the other four mercenaries were all standing at the door of the security compound. No alarms sounding, no security checkpoints had been breached, and no guards lying knocked out or dead near the compound.

"When I cut the connection this compound will be literally isolated from the rest of the compound. No alarms or safeties will go off externally." Kine told the rest.

"The internal alarms will sound. There are twenty roaming guards and forty standby guards in the compound. So sixty men total is all we have to deal with." Added Demic.

"Most important." Braco began to say.

"No blood, no body parts. Enough said." Kine cut the alarm and as he turned toward the entrance, he looked to see where the door had been pealed away from the lock and off its hinges. The door was lying several feet away from the entrance. One by one the mercenaries entered the building. By now the alarms had sounded and warning lights had began to beacon. Soldiers were mobilizing and moving towards the area of the disturbance. The mercenaries split up. Three went to the left of the corridor and the rest to the right. Kine, Demic, and Nayad went to sublevel two where the CUF36 bomb was being stored. On sublevel two Kine, Demic, and Nayad crept along, moving down the hall towards the containment room.

"Just around the corner is the containment room." Nayad said. Nayad was a few feet in front of Kine and Demic as he turned the corner. Suddenly machine gun fire filled the corridor. Bullets riddled through Nayad's body throwing him twenty feet back.

"We were so close. It's a shame." Demic said. "Nayad will be really mad!"

Quickly Nayad jumped to his feet and with lightning speed was at the containment room door. He was surrounded by the four guards that had shot him. Nayad quickly grabbed the first guard and snapped his neck. Using the first guard's gun, Nayad shot two more guards. The fourth guard had emptied his first magazine for his machine gun and was reaching for the second. Nayad looked at the guard.

"It's too late for that." And lunged at the guard. Demic and Kine moved towards the entrance of the containment room. Nayad had the guard up off the floor, writhing and trying to break free. The guard suddenly became limp. Demic reached for Nayad's shoulder and quickly threw him to the other side of the corridor. The guard's body fell to the ground.

"No blood!" Demic yelled. Looking at Nayad whose eyes were solid black with a fiery yellow diamond shaped pupil. His face looked as if it had a permanent snarl. Between the incisors and canines on both sides of his mouth were large fangs protruding an inch below the rest of his teeth. On his hands, his fingernails were like claws.

"My fault." Nayad said as his irregular form returned to a human shape. Demic looked at the door which was probably two inches thick and made of steel. Kine worked on the electronic keypad for a few seconds then turned to Demic and shook his head as if to say it's useless. Demic looked at the door again.

"Well I'll just do it the old fashioned way." Pulling his shirt off, Demic's skin turned grey and became thick and hard. His muscles enlarged quickly. Both eyes turned a bright red and at his forehead the skin separated as a third eye emerged. Inch long bony protrusions formed on the top of his head, down his neck, and across his shoulders. Wedge shaped claws protruded from his fingertips. With a powerful movement Demic slammed both hands through the top right corner of the door. Smoothly and almost effortlessly Demic pulled the door cleanly away from the doors locking mechanism and hinges. Returning to his human form Demic said.

"Our prize awaits."

The CUF36 was lying in a transparent container that was used to shield any radiation from being emitted. Nothing else stood between these mercenaries and the nuclear bomb. Nayad opened the lid of the container and picked up the bomb. An explosion of gas filled the room. Kine scanned the room as he sniffed the air.

"Cyanide gas."

"Not good." Nayad said.

"Let's get out of here." As Kine got the other two's agreements, all three started to move with the same speed that Nayad had used earlier in the corridor. In seconds they were all three standing outside the security door. Seconds later, Braco and the other three mercenaries were beside them.

"Is the package secured?" Braco asked.

"Secured." Kine, Demic, and Nayad said simultaneously.

"Excellent, let's return to our site." Braco looked at everyone. Suddenly they all had disappeared into the night.

***

A few hours later the mercenaries were all at the wherehouse at the pier. The mercenaries were dividing all of the equipment between themselves to take with them back to their dwellings. Weapons, ammunition, explosives, electronics equipment, and vehicles were all being separated and packaged for transport.

"I said no blood!!!" Braco slammed his fist to the table and yelled.

"Yes, I know." Said Nayad.

"It's alright." Kine said.

"Excuse me?" Braco snapped.

"With all the blood on the floor and the damage done to the guards neck, they will never be able to tell that the body had been mostly drained of blood. Besides they will be more occupied with how we removed the nuke from its container with no casualties to us."

"Fine. Nayad you can leave."

"Nayad. Tell Demic to come in here." Kine said. Demic came into the room. These three had been working together for years. There main reason for doing what they did is money and living beyond the reach of laws and reality.

"Braco. Demic." Kine said.

"I know you have both felt it." Pointing at the nuke lying on the table.

"I have not felt this for a very long time. There is a remnant of the Genosian Medallion in that device."

"The others haven't said anything." Demic said, trying to deny the fact.

"I have felt it also." Braco grudgingly agreed.

"The others weren't around during the Genosian War." Kine began.

"They wouldn't be able to detect its presence. It was shattered into hundreds of pieces and scattered across the universe. The energy blast that came from its breaking left an imprint that all of us who where there will never forget and can always feel. So you know the others aren't old enough to feel it. You both know we stopped counting our age in years. We account for our age in centuries. I am a 100,000 year old Vampyrh. Demic, you are a 99,500 year old Marauder Demon, and I have known you for over 800 of those centuries. Braco, you are an 82,000 year old Chaos Demon. The other four haven't even broken the century mark. They are infants in our world, young vampires and demons not able to control their hunger. So they are ignorant of what the medallion was. They are oblivious to its existence."

"The medallion was destroyed!" Demic said. Kine looked at Demic and Braco knowing old memories would have to be rekindled.

"No it was shattered and dispersed across the universe. Seventy-six thousand years ago the Genosian War began. Demons, vampires, angels and drakkynns all at war. Good versus evil as humanity likes so well to put it, but it wasn't that simple. Not all vampires and demons are evil and not all angels are good. The only exception was the drakkynns. Their immortality was created through light, humanity, and life. They could only be killed by the fiery sword of the archangel of war. Who is also one of the reasons the drakkynns were brought into being. The Genosian War waged heavily throughout all of the universe. The battles had already destroyed Venus and Mars' capabilities to sustain life, and Earth was well on its way toward annihilation. The battle was destroying the natural resources of the Earth. The forests were scorched, the continents were plagued, and the waters ran stagnant. Only a few thousand humans were still alive. The immortals only cared about one thing, total control of the Genosian Medallion. With control of the medallion, either side would be able to open the gates between Chaos and Reality or could keep the gates locked for all eternity. Demic and I fought to keep the gates closed, because we knew that if the gates were opened we would be thrown into a world that wanted nothing but destruction of everything in our universe, including us. You Braco were one of the Chaos Demons let loose to help with opening the gates. The battle itself was horrific; immortals and humans being slaughtered, earthquakes, volcanoes, and hurricanes destroying the earth, meteors and cosmic rays destroying the skies. At the climax of the battle the three drakkynns gained control of the medallion. Encircling the medallion, the drakkynns used the power of their immortalities together and caused an explosion of unseen force to rip the medallion to pieces and scatter them across the universe. The humans still blame all the destruction and death, the Earth withstood, on a super volcano that erupted in Sumatra 70,000 years ago. Myths and legends barely scrape the surface of the true battle because mans history could not contemplate the Genosian War and the immortals."

"But the Drakkynn has not been reborn." Said Braco.

"And if a piece of the medallion ever came into mankind's control, the Drakkynn would be reborn." Demic explained.

"The Drakkynn would be reborn as a man and would protect this universe as the others had done. Destroying Chaos and its minions. This was foretold to all the immortals."

"So I suggest we do what we were paid to do and get this thing to the one that hired us to find it. Do you agree Braco?" Kine asked.

"Yes, I am scheduled to meet our employer two days from now in what used to be the old Kingdom of Walachia. That is were I turn over the nuclear device. I will then contact both of you later in the week if any new contracts are offered. Until then we should avoid any chances of bringing to much attention to ourselves.

"Agreed." All three said at the same time. The seven mercenaries quietly and quickly left the wherehouse without leaving a trace of evidence behind. Leaving in different directions, within hours, were all scattered across the world.

CHAPTER XI

Soldiers were mobilized and an emergency order went out requiring immediate lock-down of Fort Eagle. Connor was ordered back to the base and since his team had been killed in action, Jack was requested to return with him to Fort Eagle. Connor and Jack walked into the conference room. In the room sat General Zorr and Brigadier General Ces. Connor saluted the generals.

"At ease Colonel." General Zorr said. Connor sat down. Jack began to salute, chuckled, and then just waved.

"Forgot, not a part of this club anymore."

"You can sit also Major Presson." General Zorr said.

"Remember! Retired Major, thank you." Jack sarcastically said.

"Fine. Please sit down." General Zorr getting irritated.

"The CUF36 nuclear bomb was stolen last night." Brigadier General Ces said.

"That's impossible!" Connor looked in disbelief at General Zorr.

"We all thought so too. Around 0100 hours, the security compounds defense system was severed. Isolating it form the rest of the fort. The west entrance was breached. The door was literally ripped from the building. Every one of the guards were killed. The door outside of the containment room was punctured and ripped off. Finally the CUF36 was removed from its shielding."

"How many of the infiltrators did we terminate or capture?" Connor asked.

"I will let General Ces fill you in on the details of what happened. He is in charge of the security compound."

"Thank you General Zorr. To answer your question Colonel Allan. NONE. We did not capture, kill or as far as we know injure any of the infiltrators. Almost all of the guards emptied at least one magazine. Very small blood splatters were seen in some areas, but not enough blood to even indicate a lethal injury. The guards at the containment room are the most puzzling. One of the guards neck was broken. His weapon was used to kill two of the guards. The fourth guard's throat had been ripped out."

"Was the guard whose neck was broken asleep?" Jack asked General Ces.

"No, and we know that because he had already changed out one of his magazines. Then the door was ripped away from the entrance much similar to pealing a banana. The shielding container was then opened and the CUF36 removed. What is not known is that without de-arming the safeties on the shielding container, a burst of cyanide gas fills the room within a hundredth of a second. Even with that, no trace of the perpetrators were found. With all of those things that have happened, the hardest thing to believe is that everything was done in less than thirty minutes. The guards made their 0100 hour check-in and once the 0130 hours check-in was missed, the secondary troops moved to the security compound and discovered everything."

"How could anyone pull this off?"

"We have no idea how this could be done, and even less of and idea of who."

"Thank you General Ces. If we can find anything out we'll relay the information to you." General Zorr told General Ces as he was packing up his things to leave.

"Well Colonel Allan, Mr. Presson. Anything to add or any ideas on who could have done this?"

"I could check with some of my contacts to see if they have heard anything about the perpetrators. At the very least they may be able to tell me where it may be headed. Doesn't it have a tracking device or a radioactive signature that can be detected?" Jack asked General Zorr.

"Normally, yes, such a device would, but sometime during your teams retrieval of the device, a stray bullet damaged part of it." General Zorr replied.

"So some how these mercenaries or whatever you want to call them must still be shielding its radioactive signature to prevent tracking."

"There are only a few mercenary groups that would have the capability or even the nerve to try and pull this off. It's just that I don't think anyone could do it in under thirty minutes with no casualties. I don't even think the NDS team could have done this. With your permission General, I would like to go see the security compound."

"Yes Colonel Allan and why don't you take Major Presson with you. Maybe your analysis of the site can turn up something the CID missed. If either of you find any information report to me immediately."

Outside the security compound, guards were on constant patrol. Connor and Jack arrived at the compound. Their Humvee pulled up to the entrance. They both walked to the door and could see how the locks and hinges had been snapped. About twenty feet away from the entrance lay the steel door that was almost bent in half. Connor and Jack entered the building and walked down the corridor. All along the walls were bullet marks and blood stains covering the floors. Both men turned left at the corridor following the signs down to sublevel two. On sublevel two was another long corridor. At the end of the corridor Connor and Jack turned right and stopped suddenly. In front of them was the containment room with the door ripped from its hinges. Jack looked back behind them at the steel door at the opposite end of the hall from the containment room.

"Connor, look at the door behind us."

Connor turned to look at the door. The door was completely covered in small dents from top to bottom. The walls, ceiling, and floor had also been riddled with bullets. As he glanced at the floor there weren't any blood stains until almost ten feet in front of and up to the containment door.

"How could that many rounds be fired between here and there?" Pointing down and up the hall.

"And no one hit anything. The ricochet alone would be lethal. With a hail of gunfire like this, no one could come around this corner and make it to the containment room door. Plus be able to take out four heavily armed guards and that includes killing one of the guards with your bare hands."

"Look at the door." Jack said. The door lay crumpled up on the floor.

"Not only was the door ripped away from the steal frame, It's made of steel. Right below the corner is a hole that looks like it was ripped into the door and not cut out. At least the containment room wasn't destroyed like the hallway."

"We didn't waste a lot of time getting down here, did we?" Connor asked as he glanced at his watch.

"No." Jack answered.

"It took, right at, eight minutes to get down here. Now if it took us eight minutes to make it to this door and we weren't sneaking around or under attack. How could a group of people remove door one, kill sixty guards, remove door number two, steal the nuke and leave the complex without leaving a trace behind. All of this in less than thirty minutes with roughly 16 minutes going from the entrance to here and back to the entrance. This is impossible!"

"Let's go check with the medical examiner over at the forensics building." Jack suggested.

"Maybe they have found something to tell us."

"It's in the Prichard Memorial Hospital complex isn't it?" Asked Connor.

"Yeah, it will only take us a few minutes to get there."

***

Connor and Jack pulled up into the parking lot of the forensics building. It had turned into a nice hot sunny day. Not a cloud in the sky. Connor stepped out of the Humvee and began to look up towards the sun. As he started starring into the sun, a strange warmth started to cover his body. His spine began to tingle and he could hear his heart beating softly. The thought finally came into Connors mind that his eyes were locked on the sun, yet he wasn't squinting and his eyes didn't hurt.

Jack stepped out of the Humvee and looked over at Connor. Taking a closer look, Jack was amazed.

"Connor." Jack said.

"The band saw trick was amazing at the very least." Reaching into his pocket.

"But do your realize that your eyes are completely yellow and glowing?" As he was saying it Jack tossed a pair of sunglasses across the Humvee.

"What?" Glancing back at Jack with a confused look on his face.

"Maybe you should put those on until that goes away."

Both men walked towards the doors. The doors automatically slid open. Entering the lobby Connor and Jack walked over to the security desk.

"We are here to see the medical examiner."

"In regards to what?" The security officer asked.

"It's about the soldiers brought here after the security compound break in." Connor slid his I.D. across the desk.

"I am Colonel Allan and this is Jack Presson. We are here under General Zorr's authority."

"I'll notify him immediately."

A few minutes later the medical examiner came out to the lobby. He asked Connor and Jack to come back to his office.

"Please sit down gentleman." The medical examiner said.

"Doctor, did you do the autopsies on the soldiers brought in from the security building break-in?"

"Yes I did."

"Was there anything unusual about the deaths?" Jack asked.

"All of them died from multiple gun shot wounds to the head, chest, and abdomen. That is except for two of the soldiers. Hold on for a second and I will go get their charts." Once the medical examiner left the room, Connor took of the sunglasses and looked at Jack.

"How do my eyes look?"

"There beautiful." Jack replied

"Come on smart ass." Connor snapped.

"There fine. You can take the sunglasses off now." The medical examiner entered the room.

"Here are the files. Neither of these soldiers had a bullet wound. Ones neck had been snapped and the others throat had been torn out."

"So they are what you would suspect for normal hand-to-hand combat wounds?" Connor asked.

"I wouldn't say that." The medical examiner said.

"But you said it was just a broke neck and a cut throat?" Connor said.

"No, I said snapped neck and throat torn out, because I can't give it that easy of an explanation. To begin with the first soldier's neck had six vertebrate that were crushed, not just broke, but crushed. So unless there was an 800 pound gorilla in the hall, it wasn't hand-to-hand combat. The second soldier's neck from the outer left side to the trachea was basically ripped to shreds and missing. The massive wound caused him to bleed out very quickly. The odd thing about this soldier's death was that I couldn't find any metal in the wound."

"What do you mean?" Connor said.

"What the doctor means is that when any metal cuts, it leaves pieces of the metal in the wound, no matter how sharp the blade." Jack explained.

"Exactly, so I am not able to give you any idea of what caused his wound."

"Thank you doctor. We appreciate your time." Jack and Connor stood up and left the building. Standing by the Humvee, Jack told Connor.

"Well, we have some information for General Zorr. It just doesn't help explain anything or give us any ideas of who is behind this." Connor and Jack began the drive back to the Special Operations Center. A couple of miles down the road Jack and Connor saw a large cloud of smoke barreling out of a tech center.

"Where is the fire department at?" Jack said.

"Pull over. Let's see if we can help." Connor and Jack pulled into the parking lot and drove to the far end where a group of people were standing. They were evacuating a group of people who had passed out from smoke inhalation.

"Where is the ambulance and fire department?" Jack asked the group. Someone from the group replied.

"Some disturbance on post last night has all the phone lines and alert systems compromised. The floor right below the helipad caught on fire and there has been a lot of structural damage. We don't know when any of the emergency services will get here."

"Help!" Two men yelled as they were bringing a third man out of the building.

"This guy says he saw two little kids in the stairwell headed towards the basement. While he was looking for the kids, a big chunk of concrete fell through the ceiling and trapped his leg."

"Are those kids still in the basement?" Said Connor.

"As far as we know."

"Come on Jack!" Connor and Jack ran into the building. Looking around quickly.

"There's a service door." Jack pointed down the hall to the left. Connor and Jack ran down the hall and threw the door open. The sign pointed left to basement and right to helipad entrance. Down the stairs they ran. At the bottom of the stairs were three hallways. One straight forward and one off to each side.

"You go right and I'll go left, we can then head back here and search the middle hall." Jack told Connor. Yelling over the noise of the building falling apart.

"Don't bother." Said Connor.

"Why?"

"Because they're down the middle hall." Jack looked strangely at Connor.

"Just trust me!" Connor said with a confused look on his face. Jack and Connor moved down the hall opening each door.

"How do you know they're down this way!?" Jack yelled.

"Because I can feel and hear their hearts beat. I just can't pinpoint it." Connor yelled to Jack as he opened a door.

"Clear!" Jack signaled to Connor.

Connor opened the next door and began to look around. Jack opened the door across the hall. Connor walked further into the room. The gentle sound of two heart beats growing louder. Back at the wall a little boy and a little girl huddled together. Both children were only about five years old. Connor walked towards the children.

"It's all right." Connor gently told the children. The children were extremely frightened by all the noise the building was making and the whaling sirens of the fire department as they were beginning to arrive.

"I found them." Connor yelled to Jack over the noises. Jack turned to look as Connor moved towards the children. Connor kneeled down to pick up the children. A sudden loud rumbling came from above. On the outside of the building, part of the helipad collapsed and began to fall though the building. Connor looked up as the ceiling began to break apart.

"Connor, look out!"

Connor grabbed the children and pulled them close to him, using his body to shield the children. As Jack watched in terror, something large protruded from both of Connors shoulder blades. Whatever it was quickly encased Connor and the two children. Rubble and large slabs of concrete bounced off of Connor. The debris had stopped falling and Jack made his way through the rubble towards Connor.

"Connor! Connor! Can you hear me?"

Jack stood there, waiting for some sign that Connor and the two children were alive. Jack took a step closer. The shell began to move. It started to unfold into two large wings. The wings looked like the wings of an eagle. They were black and gold, but instead of feathers they were covered in scales. Each wing was close to seven and a half feet long. The wings folded up and behind Connors back. Connor stood up holding both children in his arms and turned towards Jack.

"Are you an Angel?" The little girl looked at Connor. Connor looked over each shoulder at the wings that rested on his back. Jack reached for the little girl.

"Yes sweetie, he is an angel, but it's a secret. So you can't tell anybody." Connor placed the children in Jacks arms.

"Here, take the children out of here." Glancing at the wings he now bore.

"I'll meet you at the Humvee as soon as I can." Jack brought the two children outside to the ambulance.

"They said there was another guy that went into the building with you?" The paramedic asked.

"He was checking one of the rooms to make sure no one else was trapped. He is on his way out too." Connor came walking out of the building. No injuries or nothing out of the ordinary seen.

"Sir, you're injured." The paramedic pointed to the large rips in the back of Connors black t-shirt.

"I am fine." Connor replied.

"I was checking a room where part of the ceiling had fallen in. As I bent down to move away from a large section of hanging ceiling, I must have gotten my shirt hooked on some metal reinforcements. There aren't even any scratches." As he showed the paramedic.

"How are the children?" Jack asked the paramedic.

"They're fine, not a scratch on them. The MP over there said that some of the other kids had seen those two sneak off from their group over at the playground. Their parents will be here in a couple of minutes."

"Its time we go. We have a lot of things to do and a lot more answers we need." Jack said as he looked at Connor. Both men got into the Humvee and drove off to talk to General Zorr and update Dr. Cart on some new developments.

CHAPTER XII

Connor and Jack walked into Prichard Memorial Hospital. They walked down the corridor to Dr. Cart's office. Connor knocked on the door.

"Come in." From inside the office. Connor opened the door and he and Jack walked into the office. Dr. Cart was sitting behind his desk reading some papers. To the left side of the office was General Zorr sitting on a couch.

"Dr. Cart, this is Jack Presson, he used to be a part of my original NDS team. He is also up to date on my situation so feel free to discuss anything in front of him."

"Well, it is nice to meet you Mr. Presson. I am sure you know General Zorr." Dr. Cart said pointing over to the couch.

"Yes I do, and it is nice to meet you." Jack said.

"So Colonel Allan, how are you feeling?" Dr. Cart asked.

"And have you found out any information on the CUF36?" General Zorr interrupted.

"No General. As of yet, we have no leads to follow about the CUF36. To your question Dr. Cart, I feel fine. On the other hand there have been a couple side affects I wasn't exactly expecting or am I even remotely able to explain."

"Like what, for instance?" Said Dr. Cart with an intrigued look on his face.

"Both things, Jack was actually there and seen what happened. The first was when I got out of the Humvee and was looking at the sun. A strange warm feeling came over me and Jack said that my eyes were glowing."

"Glowing?!" Dr. Cart said.

"Just like a set of high beams on a tractor trailer, Dr. Cart." Jack reinforced the point.

"But most disturbing of the day's occurrences was when I sprouted a pair of wings while about two tons of rubble bounced off of me like it was a party balloon. And yes, I did say wings!"

"How is that possible? Humans don't even have a structure that would support wings." Dr. Cart said.

"Like everything else I have been doing is normal. Just look where they ripped through my shirt. Even though there is no sign that they were on my back." As Connor was finishing his statement, Jacks cell phone began to ring.

"Excuse me." Jack said exiting the room.

Fifteen minutes had past since Jack's phone had rang. Jack walked back into Dr. Cart's office.

"Gentleman, we have a lead. One of my contacts has informed me that the CUF36 was transported somewhere into Europe. They do not have an exact location, but they do know of two high priced expert mercenaries that just returned to their castle estate in Izola."

"Izola? Where is that?" General Zorr said.

"It is a city on the Gulf of Trieste in the country of Slovenia. It will take us a couple of days to get into Eastern Europe and then a few days to locate these mercenaries and their estate. Once we find them, we can see if they are directly responsible for the CUF36 theft or if they know who is. There is a jet on standby at Grindolph International Airport. All it is waiting for is General Zorr's order and any final equipment requests." Jack told everyone.

"May I use the phone Dr. Cart?" General Zorr requested. Picking up the phone, General Zorr dialed the number for the tactical operations hanger at the airport.

"Yes, this is General Zorr, fuel the jet and prepare for take off. You will be under command of Colonel Connor Allan. Any equipment that is requested, they are to be supplied with. He and Jack Presson are authorized complete autonomy. They will be there within the next three hours. Any equipment request will be made within the hour. You have your orders." General Zorr hung up the phone.

"We will leave immediately General." Colonel Allan saluted the General and he and Jack left the office.

***

Connor arrived at Grindolph International Airport a half hour before take off. The transport jet was sitting in the hanger. The jet had been fueled and the equipment that had been requested was waiting for Connor and Jack's inspection. Connor began looking over the equipment that he had requested. Four SAW machine guns and ten cases of ammo were packed in water tight black containers. Twenty five pounds of symtec plastic explosives were in a green container. Eight nine millimeter baby eagle pistols with twenty cases of ammo and multiple sets of tactical holsters were placed in a brown container. Several packs of large plastic cable binders were also in the same container. Two laptop computers with wireless capability and two hand held satellite phones were in there own containers. Several cases of MRE's, water purification equipment, uniforms, and boots had been packed aboard the jet.

"When was Jack Presson supposed to be arriving?" Connor asked the captain in charge of the tactical hanger.

"He should be here momentarily. He wanted me to tell you that he had to stop and pick-up some extra equipment for the mission." The captain explained.

Just then Jack pulled up to the hanger doors in his Humvee.

"I stopped to get a few things." Jack said as he went around to the back of the Humvee. Jack opened the rear door and inside was several specific items. The first was two custom made rifles. They had black composite stocks and stainless steel barrels and mechanisms. They used 300 magnum rifle cartridges and 24 caliber pointed soft point bullets. With their high powered scopes, they were excellent sniper rifles. Two leather jackets with a Kevlar lining were also in the back. These jackets were made with special holsters built in to conceal weapons and prevent detection by x-ray and metal detectors. The last thing in the humvee was a dark red waterproof container that held specialized communication equipment and four nine millimeter automatic pistols.

"Is there anything else that we are waiting on?" Connor asked the captain.

"Once we have loaded Mr. Presson's equipment, the radiation containment housing will be the last thing loaded."

"Good, let's get on board." Connor said. Connor and Jack picked up their personal bags and walked up the boarding stairs into the plane. Once all the equipment had been stored aboard the jet, the outer compartments and doors were closed and the jet was taxied out of the hanger and onto the runway. After receiving clearance from the tower, the last flight checks were made and the jet rolled down the runway and took off into the twilight sky.

Aboard the plane, Jack went over the trip details and double checked the condition of the equipment he had brought with him from EngKomTec. After seeing that everything was in order, Jack sat down across from Connor.

"It will be about fourteen hours until we land in Ljubljana, which is the capitol of Slovenia. From there we will refuel and fly into Piran which is only a few miles away from Izola. In Piran, we will pick up a vehicle and head to Izola. The estate that these two mercenaries live in is just on the outskirts of town overlooking the Gulf of Trieste. My contact says that the estate has a basic alarm system, but nothing that we can't infiltrate. Once we are in the castle, we can locate them or any files and try to get as much information out of them as possible."

"How basic is the alarm system?" Connor asked.

"From the information my contact gave me, we probably have a better alarm system on our vehicles." Jack replied.

"That doesn't make any sense. Why would highly paid mercenaries leave their estate wide open for someone to just walk in and steal what they worked so hard to steal themselves?"

"I don't foresee it being that easy either." There was a long silence between Connor and Jack. Both men staring out their windows into the night sky, the reflection of the full moon cascading over the endless ocean that lay below them.

"What?" Connor turned to Jack.

"What?"

"I know something is bothering you Jack. What is it?"

"Honestly, do you think you are up to this? I mean, come on, you were on your death bed only several days ago. You yourself don't even understand what has happened to you. I just don't want you to be my cause of death and I don't want to be your cause of death."

"I understand, and believe me when I say I am fine. Nothing is going to go wrong. I am at a hundred percent."

"Alright. I'll accept that. Well, we had better get some rest before we land."

CHAPTER XIII

onnor and Jack had arrived at the castle. They pulled off the side of the road a few hundred feet from the castle. Getting out of the car, Connor and Jack made a quick check of their weapons and equipment. Turning towards the castle they began walking towards the main gate. As they walked closer to the gate, they both noticed that there weren't any cameras or guards surrounding the fence. Standing at the main gate, Connor looked at the lock and looked at Jack with a confused expression. Reaching out, Connor pushed on the gate and it gently swung open. No lock, no alarm, just a slight screech as the gate opened. Connor and Jack walked up to the castles main entrance. Again the door was unlocked. Inside the door was a large hallway that split three ways. The side hallways went towards stairwells, one going up and one going down. Straight ahead was a large entrance way. Listening carefully, Connor and Jack could hear noises coming from that direction.

Connor and Jack burst through the large bronze double doors, no one in sight. Inside was a large hall, fifty feet long and forty feet wide, with massive white pillars every ten feet. The floor was marble with a fireplace at the end of the hall. The fireplace was twenty feet wide and seven feet high at the center of the arch. The ceiling was forty feet high with crystal clear atrium glass that let all the brightness of the Sun fill the hall. The walls were made of large slabs of thick grey stone and were covered with weapons of every civilization throughout the ages. On each side of the hall were large stone archways with stairways leading down. Along the archways was engraved "AS FOR THOSE WHO ENTER THIS HALL, WILL BATTLE FOR THEIR FUTURE, AND BE REVEALED THE PAST". Connor pointed out the inscription on the wall to Jack. Connor and Jack quietly moved past a set of pillars toward the fireplace. The silence in the hall was broken by the slide action of a machine gun loading its first shell into the chamber.

"Look out!" Connor yelled. The sound of machine gun fire reverberated throughout the hall. Out of the corner of his eye, Connor could see a man firing a machine gun towards Jack. As if the world was in slow motion, Connor moved towards Jack. Connor looked back up the hall towards the man. He could see each bullet leaving the barrel with a flash of fire behind it. All bullets seemed to be hanging in the air as if they were molded into a glass frame. Connor looked back at Jack, who had just seen the direction of the machine gun fire. Connor rushed in front of Jack and turned towards the man.

"Thud, thud, thud, thud……" A constant dull impact was heard for a ten second period. Connor looked down at the floor. There lay over thirty bullets, each head flattened, lying on the ground. His shirt and jacket tattered with numerous holes.

"Are you all right?" Looking back at Jack.

"So, an immortal." Connor and Jack looked up the hall. At the far end of the hall stood Kine.

"Very well, it will have to be dealt with other ways." Kine said.

"Demic." Kine yelled. Demic appeared from behind a pillar.

"Intruders. Welcome." Demic nodded at Jack and Connor.

"Yes, and they must be dealt with in the old ways." Kine nodded to Demic as his skin turned thick and gray. His fingernails became wedge like as his muscles grew. His eyes turned red and a third eye emerged from his forehead. Large inch long bony protrusions grew from the top of his head down his neck and across his shoulders.

"What the hell is that!?" Jack asked, not expecting an answer.

"This is Demic. And I am Kine." Kine looked at Connor and Jack. As the two looked on, Kines fingernails turned into claws. His skin turned red and leathery. Two yellow horns two inches long grew from his forehead above the outside edge of his eyes. His eyes were bright blue with a yellow cat's eye shape in the center that was as brilliant as the sun. Two large horns grew from his shoulders and a long slender tail that was tipped with a fiery green jewel softly came to rest on the ground. His face looked as if it had a permanent snarl with two long fangs that overlapped his lower jaw. The rest of his teeth were round with sharp tips that curved inward.

Demic and Kine lunged at Connor and Jack. With one punch Connor sent Demic flying across the hall. Kine was almost upon Connor and Jack when Connor grabbed Kines throat with his left hand and pinned him up against the wall.

"Very good." Kine said reaching down across his body with his left arm. With one quick swing, Kine hit Connor underneath his left arm flinging him down the length of the hall. Demic was quickly standing over Connors body. Demic picked up Connor by the shoulder and swiped his hand across his chest, ripping through Connors flesh and bones. Jack turned to run and help Connor and was grabbed by Kine. Kine pulled him close and sniffed along his body.

"You're a human." Kine looked oddly at Jack.

"I'll deal with you later." Kine tossed Jack up against the wall, stunning him. In a heartbeat, Kine was down the hall standing in front of Connor who was being bear hugged by Demic. Kine reached out with a claw and placed it under his chin. Slowly lifting Connors head up to his eye level.

"Before we destroy you, what kind of immortal are you?" Kine asked with a look of intrigue.

"I....Am....A....Man." Connor looked dead into Kines eyes. Connors skin darkened and became a diamond pattern scale that was greenish brown and raised in the center. The wound on his chest that Demic had inflicted had disappeared. Still starring into Kines eyes, Connors eyes turned bright green with an oval pupil that was blood red. His feet ripped through his shoes. The toes had formed into two large triangular shaped bony protrusions. A three inch long bony spike sprouted from his heals. The two middle fingers on Connors hands had fused into one finger. At the tip of each finger was a bony claw. The knuckles had formed one inch bony spikes. Connors knees and elbows had grown long horn like protrusions that seemed to extend from the bones themselves. An inch long bony spike grew above his nose and a line of spikes formed across the top of his head and down his spine across the thick muscled tail that had grown. The spikes grew to a length of eight inches at the center of his shoulder blades and decreased in size down to his tail. Two large black horns grew up and back from the top of his head. Connors face began to move forward quickly forming into a wolf like shape with razor sharp teeth. The ears formed into a triangular web shape. Finally two large black and gold eagle shaped wings that were covered with scales instead of feathers grew out and down along his back. With a swift and powerful movement, the wings expanded. Demic flew back against the wall. Kine stood there, motionless. Connor curled his fist and gave Kine an uppercut to the chest. The power of the blow sent Kine flying up into the air, slamming into the pillar thirty feet above the floor. Kine's body fell to the ground with a loud crash, breaking the marble floor and cratering the area. Connor walked towards Kine. Kine propped himself up with his right arm, holding out his left hand, showing no intent to attack.

"Stop, please."

Connor stopped and looked over to Demic who was standing at the side making no effort to attack.

"We did not know it was you." Kine told Connor as he turned to face him. Kine and Demic both returned to their human form.

"What do you mean?" Connor asked with a roughened voice.

"We did not know you were a Drakkynn." Kine replied.

"What are you talking about?" Connor snapped, followed by a loud piercing growl.

"Please look at your hands and the rest of your body." Kine reasoned quickly. Connor looked down. Seeing the scales, his hands, and his feet. Connor looked over his shoulder at the wings that rested on his back, and then noticed the tail that swayed back and forth. Connor began to stare at his hands again. Slowly his body returned to human form. All of his clothes ripped to shreds, except a pair of pants that were hanging on by a thread.

"What is happening to me?" Connor asked as he looked over at Jack who was just as bewildered.

"Just come with us. We will not harm you or your friend, and we can answer all of your questions." Kine motioned them toward the large fireplace that rested at the end of the hall.

"Yes, we have long wondered when a Drakkynn would return." Demic told Connor and Jack in astonishment.

Kine stood beside the fireplace. Demic sat down in a chair on the left side of the fireplace. He then motioned graciously to the chairs, encouraging Jack and Connor to sit down.

"First, let me apologize. We have defended our home for a very long time against humans and immortals, which were simply after treasure and our heads as trophies. I know you have many questions and I will try to explain as much as I can." Kine graciously offered.

Connor sat there in the chair, unable to start. Jack, on the other hand, was not bashful.

"OK, what are you? What is he? And what happened to Connor just now?"

"What is your name?" Demic asked.

"Jack Presson."

"Well Jack, I am a demon." Demic said as Jack had a guarded look on his face.

"Let us finish explaining. I give you my word. No harm will come to you. Like I said I am a demon, Kine is a vampyrh, and your friend took his form as a Drakkynn. I know that doesn't explain anything. I'm just giving you the basics. Kine will explain in detail about all of us, even human history that you would otherwise never know."

Kine looked at Jack and Connor. Then looking at Demic, he began to explain.

"I will start at the beginning. Which for both of you will be a lesson in truth. The universe you know of is what we refer to as reality. When I say we, I mean immortals. The other part of the universe is known to us as chaos. As humans have been taught throughout history, the sun, its planets and many surrounding solar systems comprise the universe. Your underworld or hell is our chaos, and there really is such a place. The immortals have been here since the beginning, fighting for control of both the realms. The battles have taken place throughout reality and chaos. Countless lives and worlds have been destroyed."

"Worlds?" Connor said with a confused look on his face.

"The easiest way to explain this is the planets humans refer to as Venus and Mars. One of the earliest battles raged for centuries on Mars. It destroyed the atmosphere, caused uncontrolled climate changes, and scared the surface of the planet. Venus was also a battle site. That is why it rains sulfuric acid and the temperatures exceed any mortal living conditions. Battles like these have raged for millions of years and the damage they can cause is unimaginable to humans. For instance, the meteor belt on the outside of Mars' orbit was once this solar systems tenth planet. All of these battles were over one thing, control of the gates between chaos and reality. These battles were fought by mortals and immortals. Mortal has a far greater meaning than the both of you think, for mortals includes mortal life on this planet and all the other inhabited worlds in this universe. Immortals include Angels, Demons, Vampires, Werewolves, Vampyrh, a few so called aliens, Gremlins, and Drakkynn.

"Why did you say Vampires twice?" Jack asked

"Actually I said Vampires and Vampyrh. Vampires are the ones so well publicized in literature. They have to drink blood to survive. The only way to kill them is to behead them or drive a steak through their heart destroying it. Vampires are the youngest of the immortals. They are a genetic anomaly between a human and a Vampyrh that bore a child together. The Vampyrh are one of the first immortals. I am a Vampyrh, and I am over 100,000 years old. We also drink blood, but it is not necessary for us to have it to sustain life. Angels are another immortal well publicized. One wing in heaven, the other in battle. Lucifer, the Fallen Star, was really cast into hell, or chaos as we call it, and rules there now. Demons are numerous. Demic is a Marauder Demon, known for their strength and endurance. There are also Chaos Demons, Wing Demons, Terra Demons and many more. Werewolves are actually shape shifters, able to change into any form. An old and experienced werewolf will find you, you won't find him. The Drakkynns, however, are a unique story. Chaos' legions were taking a toll on reality. Destroying planets, lives, and opening gates between the two worlds. At the beginning of time the Alpha's were born. These were the first immortals. Much like the Titans of Greek Mythology they were powerful and intelligent. However, unlike the Titans they weren't arrogant and spiteful. In this group were the first Dragons, The eldest angels, and also the Giants. Centuries past and harmony rang out through the universe. The immortals of today were born from the angels and Giants, but this new group was passionate and corrupt. The harmony that existed, began to be replaced with struggles for power. The Dragons were the protectors, keeping the universe from destroying itself. One of the Dragons and one of the Angels had offspring. Three of them. The three Drakkynns. Never before and never since then have there been any other Drakkynns born. What humans do not know is that whether it is a demon, angel, werewolf, vampire or vampyrh; they are just like humans. There are some that are good, some evil, and some who are torn between good and evil. The Drakkynns were the only immortals that fought purely for the preservation of light and life. This was an inherited trait from the Dragons. During the last great battle, earth was well on its way to being destroyed. Seventy thousand years ago the immortals were battling over the Genosian Medallion. It was four feet in diameter and made of a gold-like metal. One side had an engraved sun picture with three lightning bolts in the center of the sun. The other side had a blue moon engraved on it with a pentagram in the center. The medallion was one and a half feet thick and was used to open up gates between reality and chaos. At this point the Genosian War had taken a toll on the earth and had left only a few thousand humans alive. Before the battle destroyed all of the earth's life sustaining potential, the three Drakkynns took control of the medallion. Using their immortal powers combined, the Drakkynns shattered the medallion in a colossal explosion. This scattered pieces of the medallion across the universe and sealed all the gates between chaos and reality. The explosion put the earth into a nuclear type winter and is actually blamed on a super volcano that erupted in Sumatra seventy thousand years ago. Humans aren't capable of understanding how devastating the immortals and their wars can be. So, a natural disaster is how historians explain the death and destruction. When the battle ended and the dust settled, the Drakkynns were gone. And until now the Drakkynns have been unaccounted for. You have somehow become a Drakkynn." Kine looked at Connor.

"I think I know when it happened." Connor stated.

"Several weeks ago my entire special ops team was annihilated in the Amazon Basin. We were attacked without warning. Something moved with blinding speed, killing each member one at a time. There were bursts of flame that killed some of my men and scorched the area. Some type of three bladed weapon mutilated some of the soldiers and almost ended my life. That is all I remember. The next thing I am aware of is waking up in a hospital bed a few days later without any injuries, and not believing what condition I had been in."

"A Helgaus." Demic said nodding.

"Excuse me?" Connor replied.

"Your group was attacked by a Helgaus. It is a demon from the chaos realm. A foot soldier, whose sole purpose is to locate parts of the Genosian Medallion. They move so fast that they are seen as a blur. They can expel fire from their hands and use the three razor sharp claws on each of their hands, which there are four hands and arms, as weapons. The Helgaus attacked you because you had a piece of the Genosian Medallion, whether you knew it or not." Demic explained.

"Yet, being attacked by a Helgaus would not have caused you to become a Drakkynn." Kine attested to the story.

"Was there anything strange that happened?" Kine asked.

"Other than being attacked by a demon in the middle of a jungle." Connor snapped sarcastically.

"I mean, were there any other unusual occurrences throughout the course of the mission?" Kine revised the question.

"Actually, a few hours before the group was attacked, a volcano erupted. We were moving along the ridge line when across the valley was a huge explosion. It knocked every one of us off of our feet. The volcano was small with a spout probably thirty feet wide. The lava was yellow and orange as would be normal, yet a weird greenish glow was emitted from that area."

Kine and Demic looked at each other. Jack noticed the looks on their new hosts' faces. Connor in the meantime was concentrating, trying to remember anymore specifics of the situation. Then Kine began to speak.

"What happened is that when that volcano erupted, or any other natural disaster happens, the earth releases energy or a type of supernatural force. This itself can contain the essence of life's past. With that and touching part of the Genosian Medallion made you a Drakkynn. You are now one of us. Immortal!"

CHAPTER XIV

As the shock of the conversation wore off, Connor looked at Jack and both men remembered why they had arrived at the castle.

"Kine?" Connor began regrettingly.

"Yes, sir. Is there something else you would like to know?" Kine replied.

"More things than I can even absorb at this moment?" Jack said with a smirk on his face and a look as if he was still waiting for a punch line.

"The main reason we came to your home was in search of a bomb that had been removed from a military installation in the United States. Sources say that you two are among the top mercenaries in the world and are some of the few capable of such an operation. Plus with all the things that we have just been exposed to, it does explain some of the things that occurred at the compound." Connor explained to Kine and Demic.

"Yes, we were involved with the theft of the weapon that you are speaking of." Demic said looking at Kine.

"What the hell! You killed sixty men in that building." Jack yelled.

"Mr. Presson, I can assure you that neither Demic nor I killed anyone in that building. Those deaths were caused by the other five men in our group." Kine said.

"How in the hell do you expect us to believe that?" Jack snapped.

"Do you remember the Genosian War that we spoke of?" Kine said as Connor and Jack nodded.

"Neither of us has drawn human blood since that day, other than in this castle defending our lives and home. Since that day we have avoided great contact with man because we knew that no good would come of it. When that weapon was stole from your government, was the first time we had been involved in a mission that caused any deaths for several hundred years. The only reason we were there was as a favor to an old friend. He specifically asked us to go and help him, because this was an extremely important and lucrative assignment."

"Who is that?" Connor asked Kine.

"His name is Braco Kinng. He is one of the most ruthless mercenaries there is and he will do anything for the right price. He has the bomb and he took it to be delivered."

"Where? We need to know, because this is one of the most lethal weapons ever created. It could easily level a city the size of New York and if duplicated could be used to hold this planet hostage, and destroy the mortal and immortal ways of life." Connor asked, pleading for help. Demic looked to Kine.

"The bomb can't be duplicated."

"Why?"

"Because it has a piece of the Genosian Medallion in it, and that is the first piece I have encountered in well over 10,000 years. We will still help you to get the device. It was taken to the country side along Pitesti, a city in Southern Romania. We will take you there." Demic told them.

"All we need to know is where?" Jack replied.

"What you do not realize Mr. Presson is that without our help, you most certainly will die. You will probably die with our help. What we have told you only scratches the surface of the immortal world and you are about to be exposed to the most evil part of that world. I will warn you now; insanity may be your only escape, because your mind may not be able to comprehend what you will see." Kine said.

"Give us a moment to collect some things and we will be ready." Demic stated as Kine and he exited the room.

"What have we gotten into Connor?"

"I don't know, but I don't think it is going to get any better." Several minutes had passed when Kine and Demic returned through the archways. Connor and Jack stood up and followed the other two men out of the front entrance toward the main gate. Jack had ran ahead and pulled the car up to the gate. Connor walked to the back and opened the trunk. From his bag, Connor grabbed a change of clothes and put them on. Connor picked up the two Kevlar lined leather jackets and four pistols and ammo. Connor walked to the driver's door and handed one of the jackets and a pistol to Jack. Connor then offered a pistol to Kine and Demic. Both men refused.

"Those do not work on very many immortals." Demic told Connor. Reaching into his bag Demic pulled out two samurai swords, one long and one short. Each sword had a jade colored handle and smooth, scarless black blade with engravings that were on each side. The engravings extended three quarters of the length of the blade and could only be seen in sunlight.

"We brought these for Jack, because he will need a form of protection." Demic said as he handed them to Jack.

"What good are these?" Jack looked confused. With one blinding movement Demic took one of the swords and sliced through the steel bars and stone pillar that stood at the main gate. The blade looked as if it had been just removed from the scabbard. No scratches or even dust were left on the blade.

"These swords were made by an immortal to destroy immortals. They aren't from this universe." Kine explained as Connor and Jack stared at the damage inflicted by the blade. All of the men climbed into the car and drove to the airport.

The four men entered Southern Romania by plane and then acquired a civilian vehicle as to not draw attention to themselves. Since they had left Izola, Jack and Connor's minds had been replaying everything that had happened and many more questions had been puzzling both men.

"Gentleman, are there any other questions that you have. I am sure there are a few more things that you are wondering about." Kine offered. Connor and Jack looked at each other. Then Jack began.

"Why did you say that we were entering the most evil part of the immortal world?"

"Think back through your history. How many wars have plagued this part of the world? How many mad men have come to power and killed thousands if not millions of people here. In most of mankind's theological literature, is this not the area in the world most riddled with devastation from religious battles from the beginning of your written history. That is because this is where chaos began. Long before your history began, there was a war between the immortals that spanned the cosmos. The creator of the cosmos had set life into motion. From that moment on the fate of the cosmos rested in free will. Each immortal chose there own path, the most of the immortals chose to live peacefully and it created a kind of utopia. This wasn't the plan of one specific immortal. This immortal believed that the cosmos needed to be ruled by someone, Himself. He had a great number of followers. This immortal is the essence of the word evil. He is Deceit, Vengeance, Anger, and Cruelty at their highest levels and is one of the most ancient immortals. His name is Lucifer, the Fallen Star, cast from heavens glory as one of your great books describes. He was gaining power and creating a tidal wave of destruction, when one of the other ancient immortals stopped him. This immortal is known to mankind as Michael the archangel of war. He and other immortals separated the cosmos into reality and chaos, and chaos was where the imprisonment of Lucifer and his minions would be. Michael and the other immortals defeated Lucifer and captured his followers. Michael cast them into chaos with all of the strength that was possible. As Lucifer and his minions fell, they pierced the Earth and entered chaos. This doorway was sealed by the remaining immortals, and it is the only doorway that Lucifer could use to reenter reality. It is here that evil infects the air, the land and the water; longing for the doorway to be reopened. Some of the evil is able to escape from chaos; these are the ones that have helped cause suffering, famine, and war in this world. Others that have escaped are the basis for most of mankind's stories of the supernatural. Evil began and perpetuates here is why I told you that Mr. Presson." Kine finished as silence filled the air. The four men drove for the next seven hours toward Braco Kinng's estate. Nothing broke the silence between the men except for the low hum of the engine. As they approached the estate, Jack pulled the car over to the side of the road a few hundred feet out of sight.

"We can walk from here and see if there are any guards or security systems." Jack said.

"Braco's estate is guarded, but not in the manner that you think. We will all go and enter the estate just as if we were guests. Demic and I have brought along enough compensation to buy the weapon back from Braco." Kine told everyone.

"How can you be sure he will accept that?" Connor asked.

"We have known Braco for a long time and he has always gone to the highest bidder. Money is the only thing that matters to him." Demic told Connor. The four men walked up to the main gates. There at the front entrance was a security camera. Kine reached out and pushed a button on the wall.

"May I help you?" Came from a speaker box just above the button.

"Yes, please tell Braco that Kine and Demic are here and would like to discuss something with him."

"One moment please." Came from the speaker. A few minutes had passed when a voice came back across the speaker.

"Welcome sirs, please proceed to the front entrance and let yourselves in." A beep came from the speaker and then silence. Connor, Jack, Kine and Demic walked through the gate and up to the main entrance. Kine opened the door and walked through first followed by Connor and Jack, Demic entered last as if the two were shielding Connor and Jack. Inside the door was a long hallway. The walls were covered in tapestries and paintings. There were several elegant tables along each wall with a wide variety of collectible items such as weapons, fine art, and hand crafted clocks. Half way down the hall was a door on each side. The door on the left led to a gourmet kitchen designed in black marble and stainless steel. Through the door on the right was an entertaining room with several chairs and couches and large wine storage and bar at one end with a nice subtle fireplace at the other. The four men proceeded down the hall and through a large entrance way. Inside was a sort of staging room that was used for business deals and was definitely the wild card in a negotiation. The room was thirty feet by thirty feet with a large burning hearth in the far left hand corner. The right wall was itself a large sculpture depicting a tortuous battle of monsters and men. Within the sculpture were volcanoes erupting, lightning piercing the sky and stars falling into dark seas, all surrounded the multitude of warriors. None of the men had the same features or weapons and all of the creatures were just as different and diverse. In the center of the room hanging from the ceiling was a large colorless crystal that was four feet long. This crystal reflected the light that entered the room through the four large domes that sat at each corner of the room. At the head of the room was a large stone desk and a black steel chair sat behind it. Beyond the desk was a large black mirror that seemed to cast no reflection of anything in the room.

"Kine. Demic." Braco said as he appeared without warning.

"Where the hell did he come from?" Jack said with a startled look on his face.

"Excellent question sir, but seeing as you are in my home, maybe you should tell me who you are." Braco replied.

"These men have come with us Braco. They are looking for something that we had taken and need to return it to their government." Kine started explaining.

"You mean they have come for the CUF36 that we stole from Fort Eagle." Braco interrupted.

"Yes, how did you know that?" Kine asked with a confused look on his face.

"I knew they would come for it, although I am a little puzzled of how you are helping. But that doesn't matter. What I need from that ingenious piece of science has been removed." Braco reached across his desk and pushed a button. From within the desk a door opened and the CUF36 was raised up to Braco's reach on a little platform. Braco then motioned for someone to come and pick up the bomb. Connor went to the desk and grabbed the bomb. Connor turned to walk back towards the other men and noticed that the CUF36 was much lighter than it had been.

"What is missing from the bomb?" Connor asked Braco.

"I believe it is what you would refer to as the core." Braco said

"Are you crazy, that thing could contaminate a city?" Connor snapped.

"Silly man." Braco smirked and shook his head. With one powerful swing of his arm, Braco sent Connor flying across the room and slamming into the wall, and the bomb skidding along the floor. Knocking Connor unconscious, Braco turned towards his desk with his back to the men.

"My whole reason for stealing that bomb was for what was in it. Not what it was capable of doing. I knew a part of the Genosian Medallion was in that device long before you and Demic realized it at the wherehouse. For over seventy thousand years I have been trapped in this world, given the mission to acquire a part of the medallion." As Braco explained this to everyone, Connor woke up. Jack went to help Connor up. None of the men realizing what was happening. Braco's back was still turned to all of the men. His hands lengthened and turned into serpents. The sides of his suit ripped open as long muscular arms that had only three clawed fingers extended into the air. From the front of his chest two large horns curled up and back. The rest of his chest had large black and tan slabs of rock like material covering it and wrapping around his back. His neck began to elongate and turned into the head and neck of a serpent. Braco quickly turned around.

"That piece of the Medallion is on its way to help begin the destruction of this pitiful reality. It is a shame that none of you will be alive to see it." As Braco finished the four domes on the roof closed and the crystal shined brightly, illuminating the entire room. Braco's lower body began changing into a scorpion's body and the tail was long and spiked. Suddenly a rush of demons and vampires entered the room. The four men stood in the center of the room with their backs up against each other; surrounded.

"Mr. Presson, do you have the weapons that we gave you?" Kine looked over at Jack.

"Yes."

"Do not hesitate; your life will depend on it." Kine told Jack as his skin turned red and leathery. The yellow horns grew on his head and the two large horns emerged from his shoulders. His face turned into a permanent snarl with two large fangs and round pointed teeth. The long slender tail with the green jewel tip rested on the ground, and his eyes turned a glowing blue with a sun bright cats eye center. Looking over his right shoulder, Jack could see Demic's muscles swell and the inch long bony spikes form on the top of his head down over his shoulders. The wedge shaped claws once again tipped his fingers.

"Connor, it is your time to prepare for battle." Kine looked at Connor.

"I don't know how." As the words came out of Connors mouth, the greenish brown diamond scale pattern formed all over his body. The large black and gold scale covered wings grew from his back. His hands grew the bony spikes from his knuckles and the bony claws tipped his fingers only this time the two middle fingers stayed separated. A large bony spike ripped through the heal of his boots and his toes merged into two large bony spikes. From each elbow grew another spike that extended parallel from his forearm. On each knee a large horn grew up covering two thirds of his thigh. Connor's eyes turned a bright green with a blood red oval pupil, while his head kept its human form.

"Do not hesitate." Kine said once again as he moved towards three demons with blinding speed. None of the three demons had a chance to react as the first two were decapitated and the third demon had been drained of blood and his heart exploded within his chest. Demic had been jumped by six vampires that were trying to penetrate his thick grey skin with their fangs. Jack started to head towards Demic to help him when the vampires were thrown to the ground by Demic as if they were rag dolls. One by one Demic grabbed the vampires and threw them into the raging fire at the hearth. One of the vampires turned towards Jack and let out a horrendous growl and rushed towards Jack. As if instinct took over, Jack pulled the sword from its sheath and side stepped as the vampire rushed him. With one flawless movement the vampire was decapitated and burst into an eerie blue flame and evaporated into thin air.

Suddenly a large clawed hand grabbed Jack's shoulder. The sword was flipped upside down in a fluid motion as it pierced straight back along Jack's abdomen. Turning around, Jack starred into the eye of a large eight foot tall demon that was covered in spikes with four arms and one large black eye in the center of his forehead. Jack pulled back with the sword and quickly made a downward angled cut. Once again after the death blow had been inflicted, the demon burst into the same blue flame and disappeared. Looking around, Jack noticed that Kine and Demic had vanquished their attackers and no others had appeared to attack him. At the front of the room, Connor and Braco stood face to face. The look on Braco's face was pure anger and rage, his followers had been killed and now he himself would finish the job. Braco lunged at Connor and grabbed him with both arms.

"You will be the first one, but don't worry your friends will be following." Braco said starring into Connors eyes. Braco began to squeeze Connors body. Connor let out an agonizing yell as bones were heard being crushed. With a powerful throw, Braco flung Connor into the burning hearth.

"No!" Jack yelled running towards the hearth. Kine and Demic quickly grabbed Jack.

"Wait, it isn't over." Kine told Jack.

"My dear friend, I am afraid that for your other friend it is over, as it soon will be for you three." Braco told the men moving towards them. From the hearth came a low toned growl.

"Apparently the fire didn't agree with your companion." Braco said looking over his shoulder. The reflection of the fire shown brilliantly in his eyes. As he looked at the raging fire in the hearth, he noticed something moving.

"And from the fires of hell, is born the destructor of Chaos." Kine said as he repeated a phrase from an ancient prophecy. The movement at the center of the fire turned into the figure of a man moving towards the edge. Connor emerged from the fire in human form encased in flame. As he stepped away from the hearth, the flame receded into his skin and disappeared. Braco starred with bitterness, contempt and rage.

"I don't know who you are, but I will make certain that this time you die." Connor looked up at Braco as he finished his statement.

"No. You won't." As he shook his head, Connor's eyes turned to a fiery emerald green with a oval pupil that was blood red. The dark greenish brown scales with the raised centers covered his body. Large bony spikes grew from his elbows, back, shoulders, and knees. His hands became webbed and the two middle fingers fused into one finger and his knuckles and fingertips became hard bony spurs. The toes on his feet merged into two black bony spurs and his heel formed into a large black spike. From his shoulder blades emerged the large black and gold, scale covered wings. Two black horns grew from above his ears and his ears grew into large triangular webbed shapes. His upper and lower jaw moved forward into a wolf-like shape with large fangs and thick sharp teeth. Between his eyes grew a bony spike and then a line of bony spikes grew out from the center of his forehead back across the top of his head connecting to the same spikes that had grown from his backbone. The spikes were eight inches long at the center of his back and became smaller as they moved outward and down towards the large thick tail that rested on the ground. As the change was going on, Connors height grew to a towering fifteen feet.

"A Drakkynn! It's not possible." Braco said with a stunned look.

"You will still die." Braco said as he moved with blinding speed towards Connor. Braco charged into Connor and dead stopped as if he was hitting a brick wall, Connor had not budged while the walls and the floors of the building trembled at the incredible force that dissipated throughout the grand room. Connor reached down and grabbed Braco by the throat and held him up into the air. The other two serpent heads began biting all over Connor only cracking and breaking their teeth off on the hard scaled skin. Connor threw Braco across the room and up against the huge sculpture of the war. As soon as Braco's body touched the floor, Connor was already standing over him. Connor picked Braco up with both hands, his body limp and heavily damaged. With an ear shattering growl that made Jack, Kine and Demic all cringe; Connor threw Braco to the front of the room towards the large black mirror that was behind the desk, but instead of breaking the mirror, Braco's body vanished. Connor looked down at his hands as he morphed back into his human form.

"Where did he go?" Connor asked. Kine looked at Demic.

"It's a portal, a door way to Chaos." Kine told Connor and Jack.

"Then that is where I will go. I will finish this." Connor said as he ran towards the black mirror and disappeared into it. He was quickly followed by Kine, Demic and Jack. As Connor emerged through the portal, he was overwhelmed with the world before him. The sky was red and scorched, with a dark gloomy haze that covered the land. The land itself was dark with no truly discernible colors among the jagged razor sharp landscape. Little vegetation grew and what did grow were huge trees that were widespread and towering into the sky. Nothing lived under the huge shadow that these trees cast over the land. Large pools of grey oil like water were scattered across the landscape. Endless trails of green and purple fire spread throughout the land receding into the ground and then blazing into the air as if it were alive. Bursts of similar looking flame shot into the few forsaken clouds that were trapped above the numerous volcanoes that spewed an eerie green and black magma. Large draconian beasts flew through the sky in constant battle over the territory that they each claimed. These beasts lived in large caves that rested along the slopes of the many volcanoes. Large gargoyle like creatures roamed in herds over the vast landscape, scavenging for food and cannibalizing the weakest among them. In the distance was a huge castle made of a smooth black marble like material. Within the reflection of the marble were ghostly apparitions. There were five towers that reached high into the sky, at each of the five corners of the castle. The only entrance to the castle was a large archway, and from the distant view, the archway was the mouth of a grief stricken howling face. A long drawbridge spanned the moat that encircled the castle. On the outside of the castle moat laid a city that was just as despairing and dark as the rest of the world it was in. At the entrance to the city was a large obelisk that had three engraved letters on it. The letters were a "T" an "S", and "I". In the distance behind the castle, lay an army. The army looked as if it was training and recruiting for a much more cynical purpose than the protection of their world. Connor starred, wondering and fearing all of the possibilities that this new realm had brought to his mind. Almost an hour had passed before Kine emerged from the portal.

"Where have you been?" Connor asked.

"Before I could tell you, you entered the portal. These are doorways between two worlds, and time here is not the same as time on Earth. I entered the portal only ten or fifteen seconds after you and Demic and Jack only seconds after me, and that is why they have not arrived yet. And even once we return to Earth, days or maybe even weeks will have passed." Kine explained.

"How is that possible?" Connor said in disbelief.

"Look around you. This world is your world's hell, the underworld. An outright battle here would take the lives of many warriors from both sides and no ground would be gained. This place thrives on evil, carnage, and destruction. A battle here would cause this world to flourish and take so many resources away from ours. This is why we must leave chaos to itself and rid our world of any evil that enters it." As Kine was finishing, Demic emerged through the portal and a few minutes later so did Jack.

"Mr. Presson, look hard and remember this for all of your life and make sure your descendents know about it." Kine told Jack.

"I don't understand?" Jack looked at Kine.

"You are one of few if any mortal that has been to hell and will return. If the gates between chaos and our world are ever opened, all that you see here will overrun and infect Earth and everything else in its path. There are few mortals in our world that know of this and what could happen, but you have seen first hand what is trying to escape into our world. So prepare those that you can." Kine replied.

"It is time to go." Demic said as he pointed towards the sky. The other three men looked to see the circling dragons above them. The four men quickly entered the portal, returning back to Earth. Connor and Jack forever changed, scarred, and filled with the knowledge of Earths possible fate to come.

CHAPTER XV

One by one the four men returned through the portal. Kine and Demic stood in front of the portal

"We don't know what you are each thinking or what mental stress that has just been placed on both of you men. The only thing we can offer is the possibility of a better explanation and the reassurance of your sanity." Kine told Connor and Jack.

The four men began the trip back to Kine and Demic's castle, where they would prepare for the journey back to Fort Eagle.

***

The four men arrived at Grindolph International Airport. It was two in the morning and a humvee waited outside to take them to Connor and Jacks company. The humvee pulled into the parking lot of EngKomTec, and the four men entered the building. The building was comprised of three main floors. The first floor was a large workshop for design and production. The second floor was storage, supplies, safes, and a security area. The third floor was living quarters. It had four bedrooms, a weight room and game room. The main living area was a huge loft with an entertainment room, kitchen and dining area. First thing this morning, they would go to General Zorr and discuss the things they had seen and now knew.

At first light Jack awoke and opened the blinds into his room. As the warm sunlight hit Jack, he began to get ready for the morning briefing. Jack walked into the extremely large bathroom that connected his and Connors room. Connor was in the bathroom with only a towel on. He was starring into the large mirror above the sinks. Jack waited patiently for a moment.

"Connor?" said Jack. Connor shook his head slightly as his gaze was broken from the mirror.

"Is everything OK?" Jack inquired.

"I've been standing here, starring at this stranger in the mirror." Connor said.

"Stranger?" Jack said with a confused look, but Connor continued as if he didn't hear a thing.

"The more I stare, the more I realize that Kine and Demic are right." As Connor starred into the mirror, the image of a Drakkynn took his place.

"Connor Allan is no more, and this image in the mirror starring back at me is just a shell holding an immense creature that I can feel crawling beneath my skin. The thing that bothers me the most is that I don't know if it is me controlling it or it is slowly taking over my mind and my will." Jack looked at Connor with a strange conviction.

"I know you well enough that nothing from this world or any other will keep you from defending and protecting what you hold dear and what you think is right." Silence fell for a few moments.

"We need to wake up our guests now and go talk to General Zorr."

"I'll go and check on them." Said Connor. Connor went to his room and got dressed. He then went to the guest room where Kine and Demic were staying. Connor gently knocked on the door and walked quietly into the room. In the far right corner was a bed and Demic still lay sleeping. Through the door immediately on the left was the bed where Kine was supposed to be sleeping. Connor looked around the room and noticed Kine over in the far left corner sitting in the large ray of sunlight coming in through the window. Kine was sitting there quietly in his demon form. His legs were crossed and his arms went down by his sides, his whole body suspended in the air by his two index fingers and the fiery green jewel tip of his tail.

"Is it time to meet your general?" Kine asked.

"Yes."

"I will wake Demic and we will be ready shortly." Kine said. With one swift, powerful movement Kine lunged up into the air and on to his feet.

The four men stepped out of the humvee and walked up to the main entrance to the Hermann Command Center. The green beret guards at the entrance saluted Connor. Connor saluted back as he escorted the other three men into the building and down the corridor to General Zorr's office. Connor knocked on the generals door.

"Come in."

"Good morning Sir." Connor said.

"Colonel."

"How's it hanging general." Jack said.

"Good morning Mr. Presson." The general said with a look of slight contempt.

"Sir, I would like to introduce to you, Kine and Demic."

"Gentlemen." General Zorr nodded his head in acknowledgment of both men.

"Colonel was the CUF36 recovered?"

"Yes General, and it was delivered to the research center on our way here. But sir, there is a lot more to this than you know. We were able to recover everything but the core."

"Where is the core?"

"It is irretrievable at this time sir. There is no human way possible to bring the core back."

"I want to know where it is now!" The general said angrily.

"Look Zorr, it's in Hell, which is not exactly a real easy place to get to." Jack smarted back quickly.

"I can still have you thrown behind bars Mr. Presson." General Zorr glared at Jack.

"Who gives a shit." Jack snapped back.

"Jack is correct general." Kine graciously interrupted.

"And just who the hell are you two anyway?" Kine and Demic looked at each other with a slight smirk.

"They are the two men responsible for us retrieving what part of the bomb that we did. They are also two of the mercenaries responsible for the theft of the bomb from Fort Eagle." Connor told General Zorr. General Zorr had a stunned look on his face, then quickly reached for the phone. As the generals hand landed on the phone, another hand rested on top of it. The general looked up to see Kine standing in front of him, never noticing him move from the back of the room.

"I wouldn't do that general." Kine said. The general tried to move his hand but it wouldn't budge. General Zorr looked down at the phone. As he looked at the hand on top of his, the hand turned a leathery red and the finger nails grew into sharp black claws. General Zorr looked up at Kines face as his eyes turned bright blue with a yellow cats eye pupil that glowed like fire. The generals face had a look of worry.

"Don't be afraid general, we are not here to hurt you. We are here to help you with a problem that is much more detrimental to your world than an insignificant weapon of destruction. Because if Chaos' army marches on earth, humanity will be lost." Kine softly said as he took a step back from the generals desk.

For the next several hours, Connor, Jack, Kine and Demic explained to General Zorr what they had seen and what they knew.

"Then it's settled." General Zorr said.

"We will recruit for a special unit to prepare for this. We can recruit from all the branches of the military and from the SAS."

"With all do respect general. Not many humans will be up to this task." Demic said.

"Then where do you suggest we look?" General Zorr said. Demic looked at Kine with a slight grin.

"We have a few possible recruits as you call them."

"I also have a few people on my list to help general." Connor said.

"Who?"

"CW5 Andre Chrisson, Colonel B.J. Smitler, and deputy Marshal Marc Mancoff. They are all ex-NDS members and I know them well enough to know they can handle this situation and it's extremes."

"How quickly do you need these men here?"

"Within thirty days."

"They will also have all special pays and equipment requests. I will also have the training center and barracks opened and stocked with your requests." The general said.

"Is thirty days enough time for us to go find the people that you and Kine want to help?" Connor asked Demic.

"That should be quite enough time, except for one of the men. With him though, he'll find us, we won't find him."

"Alright, we can leave tomorrow." Connor said.

"The plane will be waiting for you and it will be supplied." The general said as the men left to go back to Connor and Jacks building. The humvee pulled up to EngKomTec and the four men got out. They all went up to the front door. Jack unlocked the door and Connor looked at the other three men.

"I think I'll go for a walk."

"Is everything OK?" Jack asked.

"No, I'm just not tired, and I feel like walking around and checking out the neighborhood. I'll be back in a little while."

"Alright, we'll see you in the morning." Said Jack as Connor started walking down the street. Connor walked down to the wharf and around the different buildings. An hour or so had passed and Connor walked into a local bar on the wharf. Connor sat down at a table and ordered a beer. Resting there, he began thinking of all the things he had seen in life up until the last operation for NDS. He had thought of how amazing the world was, how different the people were, and how each day was something new. His family and friends were one of the most precious things he knew he had. He knew this world and life were worth fighting for.

"Hey mister. Don't you think your in the wrong place?" One of the rednecks at the bar said. He was a large man with a beard who was notably intoxicated. Connor looked at the man and slightly grinned. Thinking to himself Connor took the last drink of his beer.

"Why is there always someone who likes to intimidate, humiliate, and be cruel to people or things they don't know, like, or understand. If humanity does not change this, the battle will be long and difficult to win."

"Mister, your strange and we don't like that around here. So I think were going to make you leave now." The large burly man stood up and walked to Connors table and grabbed Connors forearm. Connor stood up as the man tried to pull him to the door. Except Connor didn't budge a hair. The man was almost twice the size of Connor. With all his effort the man tried once more to move Connor. Again not a single movement.

"This sir is what I was talking about. You are being mean to someone that you have no knowledge of whatsoever. So you want to be my enemy without knowing if I could have possibly been your friend. Hopefully this will change yours and everyone else in this bars attitude. Connor turned around and left his money on the table. Walking towards the door were two ten inch I-beams at both sides of the door. Connor looked back at the man.

"This is why you should be kind and tolerant to other people instead of judgmental and cruel.." Connor looked at the

I-beam. Connor reached back and punched as hard as he could. The building trembled from the foundation to the roof. The patrons of the bar all stared in disbelief. Connor was gone and the I-beam he had punched was horribly bent and malformed.

Connor had begun walking home when he passed an alley. Connor heard a loud thump and garbage cans being knocked over. At first Connor didn't think anything of it until he heard a voice from down the alley.

"Stay away from me." Connor turned and walked quickly down the alley. There was a sharp left at the end of the alley. Coming around the corner, Connor saw a tall, pretty, blonde girl with her back up against the wall. Four men were in front of her, blocking all of her ways out of the dead end alley.

"Please get away." The girl said. One of the men quickly turned and looked at Connor as he came around the corner.

"You came down the wrong alley. Buddy."

"Let her go. If not, you will regret it." Connor said. The man snickered sinisterly.

"Your in for a very bad night mister." As the man finished saying this, his eyes turned black with a fiery, yellow diamond pupil. Two large fangs grew down past his lips and large claws grew at the tips of his fingers. Connor looked at all four men and each one of them was a vampire. Seeing the men's faces, the girl ran toward Connor. The girl was only a few steps away from Connor when one of the vampires lunged for her. With one quick punch Connor sent the vampire flying across the alley and up against a dumpster.

"Now leave and don't come around here again. Stay away from dark places." Connor told the girl and sent her down the alley. Connor turned and looked at the four vampires.

"I have been to Hell and back."

"That's where we're going to send you!" One of the vampires said.

"SHHH!!!" Connor held up his finger to silence the vampire. "And now I know how precious this world is and why I am here." Connor kept talking as he walked right into the middle of the four vampires and stopped.

"To destroy all EVIL." As soon as Connor stopped the four vampires all jumped on top of him. They were all biting and slashing at Connor. With one powerful movement the four vampires went flying through the alley. The vampires quickly surrounded Connor. Fangs and claws bared, a loud growl came form each. Connor was looking down at the ground. Slowly lifting his head, a deep thunderous growl shook the ground. Connors eyes were a bright green with a blood red oval pupil. His skin turned into the diamond scale pattern. Taking off his shirt, the large black and gold scale wings grew from his back. Sharp claws grew at his fingertips and a long bony spike grew from each elbow. The vampires attacked swiftly with powerful viciousness. The attackers efforts were useless, breaking their fangs and claws trying to kill Connor. With a powerful swipe Connor decapitated one vampire. The vampire disappeared into an eerie blue flame. Two vampires then rushed Connor at the same time. Connor turned quickly and caught both vampires by the throat. Each vampire was lifted off the ground as Connors grip tightened until both vampires burst into the same eerie blue flame. Connor then turned towards the last vampire. Walking towards the vampire, Connor morphed back into human form except his eyes stayed the bright green.

"Now go! And tell them. Tell them all. I am coming and I will rid this land of all evil I see!" Connor said stopping a few inches from the vampire.

"I SAID GO!!!" Bellowed from Connor as it shook the ground and buildings. The vampire disappeared instantly into the night.

Connor began his walk back to his company. Walking down the alley and turning towards his house, Connor noticed the same girl form the alley. The girl sat there calmly, on the left side of her neck was a tattoo that looked like a type of script.

"I thought I told you to leave and never come back." Connor snapped.

"You're the one aren't you?" The girl said.

"What did you say?

"You're the One that will lead the army into Hell. That will remove evil from reality and condemn the Evil One to his eternal prison."

"Who are you? How do you know these things and what do they mean?" Connor asked.

"I've been waiting for you since the first feather fell from an angels wing. Now that you're here, many others will awaken." The girl told Connor. A car alarm sounded on the next street. Connor looked down the street. When he turned back, the girl was gone.

"Who? What was that all about?" Connor shook his head as he walked home.

CHAPTER XVI

The next morning Connor woke up to a cloudless sunny day. The sky was blue, there was no humidity, and the day was warm. Connor walked into the studio area which was a large open area where the kitchen, game room and entertainment room were all combined. At the kitchen table sat Demic eating Count Chocula and Captain Crunch. Connor snickered.

"What?" Demic looked confused.

"I just never expected to see a demon sitting at my kitchen table eating kids cereal."

"This is really good stuff." Demic replied.

"Yes it is." Connor smiled and chuckled.

"Where is Kine?" Connor asked.

"He's meditating. Are you wanting to know something?"

"Well something strange happened last night."

"Puberty finally hit." Said Jack as he walked into the room. Connor shook his head then looked back at Demic who had a confused look on his face trying to understand what Jack meant.

"There was a girl. She was blonde, skinny, tall, and pretty with some type of script tattoo on the left side of her neck. The strange thing is that she knew about me and that I would lead a war against hell." As Connor finished his statement Demic choked on his cereal.

"Did you say a tall blonde that knew of you? And your sure about the tattoo?"

"Yes." Replied Connor

"The tattoo also looked like it had a green emerald at the bottom of the script."

"That's Arkei. She is an immortal, not like the rest of us, but no one knows a lot about her because it was thought that she was destroyed during the Genosian War. Kine might know a little bit more." Demic said as Kine walked around the corner.

"Kine, what do you know about Arkei?"

"Who wants to know about Arkei?" Kine said with a confused look on his face.

"Connor said he met someone last night that fit her description." Demic told Kine.

"That's impossible, she has been gone for centuries."

"She knew he was going to lead a war against hell, and she had a script tattoo on the left side of her neck with a green emerald at the bottom." Kine had a strange look on his face after Demic told him this.

"What's the big deal?" Connor looked at Kine and Demic waiting for a response.

"Arkei.....Legend has it that she is the deciding balance in the war between Chaos and Reality. The legend also says that the Drakkynn will loose his heart and soul and destroy all within his path. She is the reason." Kine said.

What exactly is this legend or prophecy?" Connor asked.

UNTO THE LIVING EMERALD
THE DESTRUCTOR OF CHAOS
HEART AND SOUL ETERNAL SACRIFICE
REIGNS FORSAKEN FALLEN STAR
NEVERMORE THE LIGHT TO SHINE

Kine recited the prophecy.

"Which means that Arkei will destroy the Drakkynn and Lucifer will rule all." Demic told Connor.

"So if she has returned we need to find everyone and prepare for this war. It is going to come soon. You may also have to destroy Arkei before the war begins. If not, everyone may suffer an eternal hell."

All the men left the kitchen and went to their rooms. Each man gathered the supplies that they wanted. The men climbed into the Humvee that was parked outside. The Humvee pulled up to the hanger. As they unloaded the Humvee, Demic noticed that Jack had brought the two swords he had been given. Demic looked at Jack with a slight smirk. Jack noticed the look on Demic's face.

"Hey. It's nice to have a weapon that works." Jack said to Demic as he shrugged his shoulders. The men boarded the jet. First stop, the head of the Amazon River.

www.ingramcontent.com/pod-product-compliance
Lightning Source LLC
Chambersburg PA
CBHW061547310726
48972CB00008B/2655